Phoenix:
Field of Mars

Jackie Anders

Black Rose Writing | Texas

First printing

ISBN: 978-1-68433-164-2
PUBLISHED BY BLACK ROSE WRITING
www.blackrosewriting.com

Printed in the United States of America
Suggested Retail Price (SRP) $16.95

Phoenix: Field of Mars is printed in Chaparral Pro

This book is dedicated to my grandfather,
Elder L. Reddoch (Das), for showing me what God's
love is really like through his example and care for me.

Special thanks to the Warrior Bonfire Program
(warriorbonfireprogram.org)
for their steadfast support and to all our
veterans/currently active soldiers for their service.

Phoenix:

Field of Mars

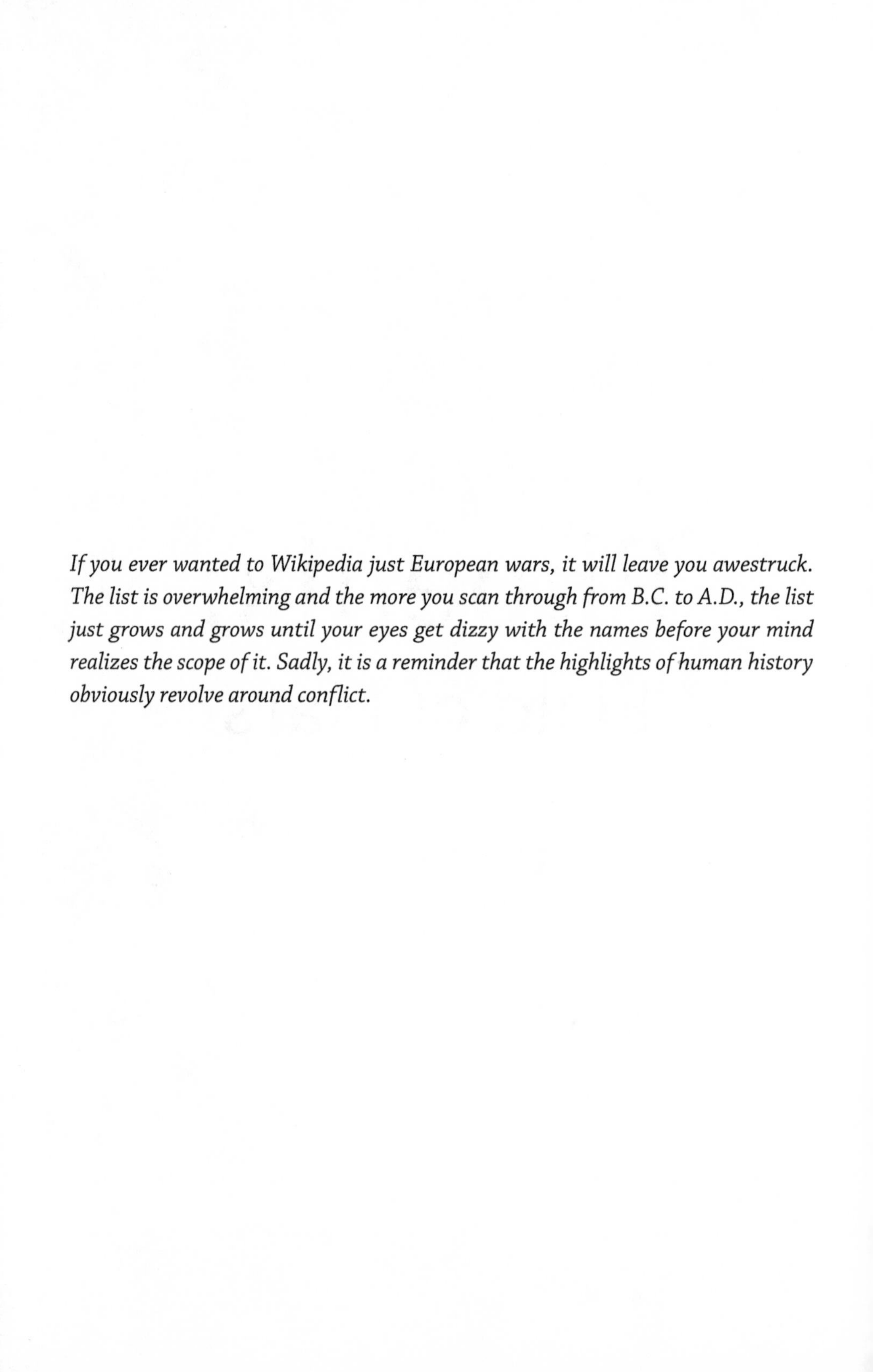

If you ever wanted to Wikipedia just European wars, it will leave you awestruck. The list is overwhelming and the more you scan through from B.C. to A.D., the list just grows and grows until your eyes get dizzy with the names before your mind realizes the scope of it. Sadly, it is a reminder that the highlights of human history obviously revolve around conflict.

Chapter 1

On the beach in La Concha, soaking up the sun, would have been way more preferable than being trapped in a dungeon. Or at least a prison of my own making. But I needed to count my blessings, because I was safe inside West Bank Labs, one of the many businesses my new clients owned outside of America. Unlike the day before, when I had first arrived on the volatile streets of Israel.

Getting to the labs from the Ben Gurion International Airport in Tel Aviv, Israel, had been a huge wake up call for me. Heck, as soon as my driver pulled away from the curb of the airport, thunderous vibrations skirted the atmosphere all around us. The compact car shook with each explosion sending me down onto the floorboard cowering like a child. My driver paid no mind to the warfare outside. "Palestinian mortar attacks," he told me. "No worries. We're fine here. We're about twenty-five kilometers away from all that, give or take." Either way, I didn't sleep much in the hotel that night.

The shaking blinds on the opening office door signaled that my boss, Walter, had arrived to the labs for our morning meeting. His abrupt intrusion snapped me back into business mode. Walter had some new blue shadows under his eyes. I wanted to ask about his night but held my tongue. He opened a legal length file and spoke without looking up at me, "Kyla, grab me that file on the table behind you. The one they left for us with all the construction permits. There's something in there I need you to see."

I did as he instructed but asked, "A hostile area in a foreign land? At least tell me the coffee is good."

He didn't answer. The tension was suddenly so thick I could make a malt shake with it. I pulled my long brown hair up off my neck and into a hairclip.

It was time to get busy. I had worked for Walter for six years. It became easy to gauge his moods. He was worried about something. And I knew this client was important to him, because I had been informed of the trip just a few days before back in America. Three days later, we had arrived. We were across the vast Atlantic Ocean far from home and sitting in an office with windows overlooking Ha-Notrsrim Street in Israel. Israel of all places. Don't get me wrong, Israel was a neat place in its own way. Not counting the war zone aspect. And it wasn't that it was aesthetically pleasing either. Just that it was rich in culture and history. So many things happened in Israel. So many wars.

My navy blue suited boss fidgeted with his tie before bringing his slate, grey eyes to mine. "Kyla, I think you'll live. But yes, the coffee is good. You know, this place could be neat to tour if we weren't so busy this time." Ah, he was capable of a little reprieve from all the gloom. It was nice but short lived. "Maybe next time."

"Yea," I said. But Jerusalem? Yea, maybe. After all, it is where Christians claim is the site for the death of the son of God, Jesus. My mom was Catholic, so I was apprised of many of these facts. However, I knew Walter picked me to assist on the project because I was also part Jewish. Jewish on my dad's side, that is. But I didn't think it relevant for our clients, who ran a space exploration company, to be here and needing me, our services, or anything like that in this part of the world. It was all rather odd. Odd and puzzling. On any count, it did pique my interest.

"Now, see this?" Walter asked sharply. Moving abruptly around the conference table toward me, he carried some kind of legal document in his hand. He shoved a rolling chair out of the way as he descended upon me. "This is why we're here."

I took the document from him as he continued, "Our clients cut a few corners that they have acknowledged to us. I don't think it's too big of a slip up. We've worked with ones like this before, so I'm not worried yet..." He stopped short as a dark skinned, young lady walked in.

She offered him some papers with a timid smile. "More like you requested," she said speaking English but with a strong Israeli accent.

Walter paused and rubbed the back of his neck. "Just set it there." He watched while she placed the file down and exited the room. Then, he circled back to me pointing at the paper. "Look at this, Kyla. I need you to sink your hands into it and tell me what ideas you get out of it. We're running out of time before the press gets to run with this."

He stepped back to pick up the new file and flip through it. "So we have two meetings today with legal and three tomorrow with zoning. Also, don't forget the eight o'clock at the Embassy and the ten o'clock with Alfred, our client's liaison." He pulled out his iPhone. "I'm synchronizing all this to your calendar."

My demanding boss, with his clean shaven face and well-groomed eye brows, stopped on that thought and glanced around preparing to add a whole list of other things for me to do. Walter was well in his fifties and not one to cross. He had been married two times and both didn't work. Even though he was athletically fit and barely greying, I was glad he looked at me more as a daughter than his next venture. The only thing I wanted from him was his job.

The furrowed brows over piercing deep-set eyes woke me from my sordid thoughts. "Did you get all that?"

I nodded.

"One more thing Kyla, our client is getting push back from both the Israelites and the Palestinians." He clasped his hands together and gave me an even more pained gaze. "Therefore, not only is our client's image on the line, but two governments getting involved is something to worry about too."

That is true. And from my knowledge of history and many years of viewing CNN and Fox News, I knew all about the constant strife between those two countries. But in particular, Jerusalem, most of all. The Israelis and Palestinians both claim Jerusalem as their capital.

"What are you not telling me, Walter?" I asked while tugging at the small diamond stud in my ear, an ongoing nervous habit. I had yet to see on the paper exactly what he was referring to.

He closed his file and rested his ringless hand solidly on top of it. "Basically, it all started because Stellar Solutions changed part of its Mission Statement on *all* of their subsidiary companies, including their branch here, West Bank Labs, to read '*unknown exploration*'."

I tilted my head to the side. My neck muscles had my head in a vice from my restless night. "Unknown exploration? Oh, so that is why both Israel and Palestine freaked?"

His wire rimmed glasses dropped to the desk as he looked back down to scrutinize the rest of the reports with a shrug. "Yep, the slip up by Stellar Solutions' management team of adding just those two simple words, doubled with the fact that some fresh out of college lawyer caught a discrepancy in our client's application for construction permits,...is all now causing chaos for West Bank Labs."

I picked up another file. "So, let me make sure I have this straight. West Bank Labs is in trouble because their father company, Stellar Solutions, added to their corporate goals something odd about wanting to do some form of science exploration? On top of that, they messed up their permits for this lab. Do I understand all this right?"

"Yes."

"Okay. Yea, that's a lot of screw ups." The papers before me looked daunting as I flipped through a few. What angle would the press take with all the heightened emotions of the people here? "You know, I can see why a space exploration company setting up a new facility out here, no matter how they originally initiated it, would draw some negative attention to begin with. Honestly, I wonder how they even got this far, don't you?" I said it without worrying about his reaction, which surprised even me.

Walter breathed heavily through his nose. "You know how this goes Kyla, don't let those details grow teeth. Worry about how to counteract those same questions you're asking. And do it quickly before the press takes liberties without us." Picking up his glasses he continued, "They only gave us till Sunday. So remember Kyla, when our clients mess up, it's our job to fix it!" In no time flat, he was out the door with one of the files tucked under his arm.

"Ouch," I thought. I struck a nerve. He had seemed a little sensitive all of the sudden toward me. Was it because I was questioning our client or questioning him? Well, that's lovely. Now it was time to redeem myself. I knew then that I would be working late all week in a strange facility, but I was going to have it solved before Friday. If anyone was going to pull a rabbit out of a hat that soon, it was me. I was always an overachiever.

I flew through my degrees quicker than most. When I graduated college, I had big ambitions. I spoke five different languages and possessed a Master's degree in International Relations. After a few short years, I made it up to the executive level of a Fortune 500 company and later became a Public Relations

Assistant Director at the age of twenty-seven. It didn't bother me that I didn't have a life or was never married. I didn't need a man. I was thankful for the accolades and the no time for vacations kind of life, or was I?

****

Midnight came and no matter how hard I tried, I still couldn't PR that mess just yet. I needed food and fresh air to clear my mind. I left the building with an escort in hopes of something being open late.

"Still working, huh?" asked my appointed guide who greeted me outside the building. He spoke nice but something about him made my breath short. He had wrinkles carved through out his dark face and around his coal-colored eyes.

"Always," I said before putting my hands into my pockets. I kept my words short and the conversation light just in case. Maybe, it was his unfriendly stare. It also didn't help that Middle Easterners were always portrayed on television as evil and potential terrorists. The narrative was always the same. Always stating that they were against us. However, Stellar Solutions was a big conglomerate corporation. They had plenty of money to hire trust worthy escorts. I pushed the nervous thoughts back and followed him down the narrow cobble road.

A few rough steps and there in front of us was Amigo Emil Restaurant. He turned to me with a half smile. Finally, portraying kindness. "By the way, my name is Pedro, Mrs..."

"It's Ms... Ms. Kyla Marshall, but you can just call me Kyla."

His thick eyebrows gathered in the middle. "Nice to meet you, Kyla." He turned and pointed at the small establishment. "This here is the best diner in town. What do you think?"

"Looks perfect!" Amigo Emil Restaurant was just as cozy on the inside as it looked on the outside. Walking through the small door frame, I immediately noticed how the interior walls were made out of stone. Not just any stone, but ones that looked to have a marshmallow texture with snowy, mountain air paint colors splattered all over them from floor to ceiling. The ambiance was so romantic all around with dim lighting and soft instrumental music playing. It actually made me wish I was attending with a boyfriend, fiancé, or even a husband. The thought was fleeting, because I knew my career came first. And no matter how many elegant restaurants I attended alone, it wouldn't change that fact.

My date for the night, Pedro, sat at the bar while I was seated at a wooden table in the corner. I declined wine, which I hated to do, but I knew I had more work to do tonight. A nice lady came to my table, and I hungrily ordered lamb chops with rice and a cup of coffee. The coffee came out within minutes in a dainty blue floral cup and tasted heavenly. Sipping my coffee felt so good this late. It was just what I needed after a stressful day.

There were black and white pictures adorning the walls all around me. Portraits of women in headdresses and men in suits. I wondered if they were related to the current owners or even me in some distant way. I didn't get to meet many of my father's family. Most died before I was born, or he didn't have much of a relationship with them. In fact, I didn't have much of a relationship with him either. Before my parents split, he was always at work. He died not too long after they divorced, but we didn't attend the funeral. I always thought it was because my mom hated him. She had just told me it was because the funeral was overseas, and we couldn't afford to travel there. I still think about him from time to time. What would it have been like to have known my father? Would I view men differently? Being here in Israel made me even more curious about him, and my thoughts swirled around thinking about the stranger I called Dad.

The meal came out filling up more of the plate than I was prepared for. The sizzling scent was still surrounding the pale meat. About five bites of that lightly seared lamb and six or so of the cilantro flavored rice, and I was done. Full and content, I felt the weight of my day rest on my eyelids. So I ended up calling it a night after dinner. My hotel had become my destination, not my office. I needed sleep. I knew I had a busy day tomorrow.

****

Too many emails on my phone was keeping me occupied while waiting on the stupid elevator the next morning. I had just finished an eight o'clock sharp meeting with the United States Ambassador and two of Palestine's prominent officials, Abbas Hashim and Petra Saldo, that didn't go as well as I would have liked. I headed back to West Bank Labs fidgety and needing a drink.

The elevator finally dinged once to signal that the door was about to open for me to get in. When it did open, there were four military soldiers dressed in tan desert fatigues and sporting slight beards. They stood there with their eyes fixed on me. I didn't think much of them but by the looks on their faces, they paid more attention to me than I did them.

Yep, I cursed myself for wearing my dark purple skirt suit at that moment. It was my favorite attire for office meetings. I purchased it from a Marciano store in Sidney, Australia because it brought out my brown eyes and dark hair. I loved it from the moment I put it on. It accented my best features and fit me just right. Well, clothes fitting just right was getting me the wrong attention on the elevator.

I stepped in and turned facing away from them. Soldiers didn't do it for me. I always viewed them as gun crazed and muscle building, obsessed grunts. I like my men in a suit and tie with high intellect. Men that enjoy fancy wines, golf, and maybe the occasional opera. Although that wasn't getting me Mr. Right either. Which I doubted there was such a thing anymore anyway.

Pretending not to notice their ridiculous banter, I kept my eyes glued on my emails. "*Sie ist perfekt sie,*" said the one to my right with an American accent and humor in his voice. I couldn't see him, but I knew he was smiling.

He obviously turned to the soldier on my left because that other soldier replied with a short response.

I rolled my eyes. It was just so pathetic and typical. Tired and coming unglued, I turned to the overly tall soldier on my left and surprised him with my very fluent German, "*In deinen traumen*" meaning "*In your dreams*'. I peered up at him and saw an obviously embarrassed, yet nice looking guy. He was wearing military attire, same as the others, but with a baseball cap sporting some kind of fishing logo. What a contradiction, I thought. I smarted off after that with "and pick up your jaw, that's not a good look for you."

At that precise moment, the elevator door opened, and I quickly stepped out. I grinned a big smile back at him right before the door shut between us. I could tell the other three soldiers were laughing at the victim of my rage. As the door closed, the poor guy sank his chin into his chest and laughed too. I walked over to the snack machine still gleaming from my victory over the masculine pigs, but I noticed the snack machine was empty. So, no sugar fix. I shrugged my shoulders and said to myself, "It's the small victories, Kyla. Can't win 'em all."

****

Night time came before I could make as much headway as I wanted to. As always, everyone was telling their good nights and I saying the same, "Thanks, you too." I never even looked up. It was more like a mother shooing away her kids than a co-worker saying her goodnights to everyone. I wanted to say, "Go, bye, see you tomorrow" or "Just go, you're distracting me".

Two more files to go and a few more video briefings, and it was already late. The stillness in the offices on the floor I was on was nerve wracking from some reason. I usually enjoyed the quiet. I could get a lot done. I didn't know why my unsuccessful day turning to an equally unsuccessful night had me feeling like a porcelain doll being dropped onto the hard cement. The thrift store clock on the wood paneled wall struck midnight. Where did the time go? I pulled out one more file, reached for my hi-lighter to emphasize the verbiage printed in it about physics and properties of space, and... why was that in there? Science was never my best subject. I read it the best I could. Blah, blah,... and then the last thing I remembered was my head feeling comfy laid on top of my folded arms on my desk.

****

There was a ringing sound that woke me, and it was not my alarm clock. Drool was running down my face and onto one of my files. "Is that my cell phone? Tardy bell? Am I in college still with the class bell ringing? What is that?" I thought. A snowy blizzard of film was covering my eyes so I had zero visibility until I wiped my eyes. They burned from it a little but hey, it had to be three o' clock in the morning. What did I expect? There was a ringing again and the light going on and off in my purse meant it was my cell. With a yawn and a click on the 'answer' button, the annoying noise stopped. "This is Kyla," I said with a yawn.

"Yes, Kyla?" The voice on the other end was iffy. I didn't know who it was, but they sounded a little familiar.

"Speaking."

"Go down to lab sixteen, subfloor two."

"What?"

"There is something waiting for you there that will help with Petra Saldo."

"The Pakistani critic who argued with me at the Embassy?" I stretched my free arm.

"Just do it and hurry!"

My usual self would have questioned him more, but I was tired and my bed was calling me from the hotel. I laughed at the personification in that thought and got up to go where I was told. The sooner I got down there and picked up the package, the sooner I could head to my hotel to get at least a few hours of sleep.

The elevator dinged alerting me to my arrival on subfloor two. Two guards greeted me wearing black pants and beige shirts. They opened the main door for me after I showed them my badge. They didn't say anything or ask for anything else. As I easily walked by them, I said, "Thank you. I won't be long".

The men shut the main door for the floor behind me, but in front of me still were several more doors. Lab sixteen was way farther down the hall than the rest. When its door opened with a simple push of the button on the wall, I saw that the lab was surprisingly empty. Searching the empty space for whatever was supposed to be there should not take long. I hoped. I walked down the aisle between most of the equipment until I came to the end of the room where most of the machines were.

"Hello. Is anyone here?" There was no reply. "I was called down here to pick up something. It's Kyla Marshall of H. L. Wiggins Corp. I'm one of your contractors. Someone here?" I felt stupid. Maybe I imagined the call. I was half asleep when the supposed call came. Yea, I was wasting my time. I turned to head back out, but there was a boomerang noise. I thought nothing of it at first and walked closer to the possible source in the corner of the room. It got extremely loud, similar to a high voltage sound from a low hanging power line like I jogged next to back in college. Eerie as it was, it still didn't seem foreign. I looked around. Then it got so loud that my ears screamed. All I could do was protect them with my hands and wonder about what those scientists were up to.

No one was around, though. No lab coat staff anywhere. I knew there were quite a few working on the lower level floors daily because I saw them always selecting those floors on the elevator. And even though it was my job to know all the inner workings of my client's business, at that point, I still hadn't been fully informed of their purpose in the labs. Or the reasons for their work underground. I had been through many labs with many companies that I represented. I had heard many strange noises. It had to be a typical day in a lab, right?

I removed my hands from my ears to pull back my hair into a pony tail and turned to head back to the guards when something peculiar danced around in the corner. A light. A faint light. But it was getting brighter and brighter. Or was that my ... All of the sudden it all went dark, pitch dark. I couldn't remember much after that.

Chapter 2

Days pass so fast leaving blurs of life's memories, but most washed away clean with the expanse of time. I had many good years but more that were not. For the most part, I was not upset with the loss. Some things were best left forgotten. Between my parents' divorce, my mom remarrying that jerk, and us moving around from town to town each year, there were many bad days that I didn't want to remember. And with the turmoil during the day came the frequent nightmares at night too. They were all the same with me angry and fighting something or someone.

Then, there was that one dream. The beautiful dream that I had one night during my high school senior year. The night my boyfriend of two years broke up with me and dropped me off at my home devastated. I gave that pipe dream a name; I called it my 'River Dream'. But that dream couldn't have come at a better time than that night. Because that night was when I fell to my lowest point. My boyfriend was angry. I knew when he left me, he wouldn't want anything to do with me again. It was a deep cut emotionally. Deeper than I ever felt before, even deeper than my childhood wounds. We had been so happy before that night juggling teenage life, adult expectations, and our own discoveries together. It was a huge fall for me.

As his car rounded the curve away from me, I walked and walked until I was close to the river. The great Mississippi River with all its greatness. I didn't remember how I got there so fast. I didn't live that close to the river. But I got there. I got there with a sense of loneliness that was tearing at my soul. I had had a companion. A friend. Someone to lean on. Someone that wouldn't hurt me like my stepfather or leave me like my biological father. But he did.

And as I stared at the river that night from the bank, my impulses were taking over. The coldness of the river was calling me to join the others that graced its presence throughout history but never left. I wondered how it would feel to sink down into its dark depths and never come back up. The tears ran down my cheek warm. For the first time in years, I was actually crying again. I hated myself for it. I hated that I trusted someone again to get to that point again. To *cry* again! The more I thought about it, the angrier I got and the more I leaned over.

Then, the wind blew. Hard and strong like a tuba player thrusting its sound across the stadium. I sank back to catch my balance and collapsed on the wet grass. I knew I couldn't do what beckoned me. I looked around and watched the wind blow through the trees as if speaking to me. Telling me I could pull out of this. Telling me I could move forward. I heard without ears the words "step by step", "day by day". I didn't know how I thought of them. But they were there in my mind. There just like I spoke them. And with that, I laid down with the tears now dry on my face and slept right there on the bank of the river. And in that slumber, I had my first peaceful dream. Not one of hate or anger like all the others. No, it was a sweet dream even though my heart was broken. A sweet and peaceful dream among a terrible, harsh and cold night. After I woke and for the next few years, I longed to have my 'River Dream' again.

****

"Hot, hot, ugh! What is that heat?" I was sweating just a little so it wasn't the room temperature. There was nothing around me. Just a dark room with nothing in it. There may have been a light coming from above, but my head was spinning so much that I couldn't make out what it was.

"What the hell is this?" a stern male voice behind me asked. I froze. I strained to adjust my eyes to the dark but a new fear had me shaking beyond belief so much that I was almost in tears.

"It's a woman," came a second male voice, this one a bit more pleasant. I turned to the second voice and could finally start making out the shape to be in fact a male. There were more than two though. I could make out four at least. The better my vision adjusted, the better I could see their ragged clothing, the menacing beards on their jaws, and blank looks on their cold faces. Their eyes pierced me sharply as if they wanted to tear my head off. My mouth went dry and the flight-or-fight instinct started to pulse through my veins. This wasn't good, but I couldn't make my body move. It was like I was in a nightmare and couldn't retreat. Was it a dream? Did I pass out in the lab? No, this was too real for a dream. Unless I was overdosed on something for anxiety, I could always tell the difference between consciousness and dreams. No, it was real.

My mind instantly started trying to put the pieces together as I saw my neighbors in the dark room shift to speak low among each other. Maybe I fell in the lab and hit my head? I should have woken up in a hospital though. Stellar Solutions' scientists? Maybe I stumbled in on one of their tests. No, those lab guys were always clean shaven and did not dress in rags. Or at least the clothes that the strange men before me had on were sort of ragged. For the most part, their garments were brown but hung on them like a loose gown on a woman. Or maybe more like a priest's robe, just not as colorful. Yea, that's what it reminded me of. So that didn't make sense either.

As the men conspired with each other, I feigned the will to speak, "Where am I? Who are y'all?" When the first male went to speak again was when I noticed the rifle. A rifle! What the hell? Why would a priest carry a rifle? I hated guns. Always did. Ever since I worked for a client that had a mass shooting next door to one of their facilities in France.

"No...," he sneered. "The question is, why are you here?" He then tapped his rifle twice when he realized I eyed it. I didn't know what to say. I wondered why he didn't ask for my name or my corporate badge.

"I don't know. I just guess I fell or passed out," I feebly let out. "I was called down to sublevel two for something, went down into your lab, and now here I am. I don't remember anything else."

"Is that the best you got?"

I blinked. "Yes, because it is true!"

The two speaking men looked at each other, and then looked back at me. I was in their den, and they were on the prowl.

I did what any prey would do, I tried to distract them. "Look, can someone tell me what is going on?"

There was no reply. The other two men in the room, off to my right, never took their eyes off of me. That was when I started to get creeped out.

"Interesting," was all the second male said in a more familiar way. Then he looked to and addressed the first male, "You know what you need to do."

The first male stood up with apprehension in his gait. He looked down at the second male, handed him his rifle, and then his eyes met mine. At that moment, I thought he looked slightly familiar but couldn't place where. Just as soon as that thought passed, his stare got hard and I started to break out in a cold sweat. His over-imposing size and the set in his jaw, made my fingers go numb. As he started moving toward me, I screamed and put my hands up to feebly protect myself while I tried to stand to run. There was a struggle as he grabbed my hair and then just as I noticed a sharp pain on my scalp, it all went dark again.

Chapter 3

I love the subtle tone of a violin. It's smooth, silky sound resonating in my ears. I started to come to slowly and the sweet violin's melody turned to a shuffling of paper. When I opened my eyes, I noticed it wasn't paper at all. I wasn't at any concert or in an office. I was still in that dark, dirty room. Dread hit me as I looked up to find one of the men in the group that attacked me, slowly sharpening a knife. Before I could scream, he put the knife down and whispered, "I'm not gonna hurt you. Calm down. It's going to be okay. We're friendlies, okay?" He lifted both his hands with palms up to help overt my raging fear. He knew I was terrified. "My team and I are a special ops unit contracted by Stellar Solutions. We're on your side, okay?"

Trying to stand, a stirring sensation spread across my head slowing my rise. I gave up. Stretching it with movement made it hurt worse. "I don't understand. You're not dressed like soldiers. You're dressed like hobos." Rubbing the impact spot on the top of my head seemed to help.

The man spoke again, "My name is Sergeant Banks and we are on a mission that you, for some reason, dropped in on."

Processing his words and slight southern accent, I added, "A mission? In the building? Don't you think that is a little strange? Why would Stellar Solutions hire you to spy on their own building? Or are we still in Israel at all?" The impact spot stung again and I grimaced. "Did I take a trip with y'all?" Taking in the room again revealed that it obviously did not have sheet rocked walls. Just dirt and rock.

Banks let a small smile lift up one side of his mouth and then dropped it just as fast. That was when I actually studied his face & realized he looked about my same age, maybe younger. Even with his thick beard, his face still looked boyish. Hidden deep under a dirt smeared canvas, I could see dark brown eyes even though there wasn't much light in the room.

He then moved his upturned flashlight closer to us. I guess to gauge my reaction to what he was about to say. But when the light shown more so across his face, I took in the rest of his physiognomy. His thin lips turned up slightly in both corners gave him a sweet, rather handsome appearance even when he wasn't smiling. As grave as he acted, Banks still had a genuine aspect to his features.

Then, he twitched his lips and looked down for a second. I could tell he was thinking of what to say next. Almost like he wanted to soften the blow for me. With his gaze set back on me, I could finally discern from the softness in his eyes that he wouldn't hurt me like the soldier from earlier did. He nodded. "Yea, I guess you can say that. Actually, the latter would be more of the truth."

He paused again for a second and then continued with a gruffer tone, "Ma'am, what I am about to tell you can't be helped, but it will take you off guard. However, you still need to know this if you are going to survive." At the word 'survive' my mouth gaped open. "Stellar Solutions isn't just any space company. It has found a way to travel in time. You are not in 2017 anymore. You are somewhere in the year 8 A.D." Banks raised his hands up to me again like he was preparing for me to dash out.

I didn't dash, I froze. I didn't question or laugh or cry, I just froze. And even though that all sounded crazy, the foremost thing on my mind was, "Okay, so what are y'all planning on doing with me?"

Banks laughed. A quiet laugh, but still a laugh and said, "You must be from the South".

I flicked my gaze back to him. "Excuse me?"

"You're a knot head."

"Knot head?" I asked. I opened my mouth to criticize. Then, stopped short when he grinned again.

Shaking his head with a smirk, he began to rise. "Never mind. Listen, when I bring you up to the top of this cave..."

"Cave?"

"Yes, cave. You will see that I'm not joking. Also, you will see that in order to stay alive, you have to trust me and my team."

My body temperature rose a few degrees. "And that was exactly how I felt when one of your team mates attacked me earlier."

"Oh, that is Captain Eriksen. He's not all that bad. He's a Norwegian so a little butch-like, having Viking blood and all. But truth be told, he originally planned on killing you and must have changed his mind when he approached you."

My throat started to burn. "Kill me? My God, what is going on? Are y'all still planning to kill me?"

"No." Banks turned to put a few more things in his bag. Then he handed me a canteen to drink, which I took hesitantly. I knew I had no choice but to trust him. "The mission is already underway. I stayed behind to watch you while you were knocked out since Eriksen pointed out afterward that killing you would further complicate things."

"Well, I'm glad to be a complication," I finally let out the breath I was holding so I could get serious and on Banks' level. "So why you? And what is this mission they are on?"

"To monitor you. I'm the only one on the team with medical training." He winked. "And to be honest, I can't tell you much but just that one of Stellar Solutions' scientists came back to this time to do something that would cause a lot of problems to our time. We were sent in to stop him contracted by Stellar Solutions and some higher ups at the United Nations as well. But we were sent back to the time that he originally traveled to. Because we can't travel within our own century, we had to work in the confines of what the machine would allow."

So there he was with that time travel nonsense again. I just shook my head like I understood and thought maybe if I kept prodding, the truth would come out. But as I was about to ask my next question, I heard sounds coming into the room, or cave as Banks called it. It was the soldier that hurt me earlier, Eriksen. There was reddening building on his angular face and a sheen of sweat on his forehead.

I cowered to the back of the room in hopes to hide, but I knew it was futile. His attention was on me before I could look away. Now that my eyes were more adjusted, I could tell he was a force to be reckoned with. He stood way taller than me. Huge even. Where Banks was probably close to six foot, this Eriksen was easily way over that. He was real muscular like Banks but broader shouldered.

I took the risk to gaze back up at his eyes when I noticed they were a bright blue like the waters off of Key Largo beach. That was about the only thing nice about him. He scared the crud out of me. Even his wildly, blonde hair and rugged dirty blonde beard were disturbing. I could see it clearly when he took his hood off to urgently address Banks, "Get out here. We need to talk." He spoke in English but had a different accent that I could tell he worked hard to cover up. It sounded more like what I had come across on my work in Germany or Sweden. Which made sense since he was from Norway.

At that Banks & Eriksen left the room. I knew I should stay put without being told. I heard them right outside the room talking louder than I figured they would. I also heard the other two soldiers conversing with them as well. I couldn't completely make out what they were saying, but I prayed it wasn't about me. Maybe I should just slip out and disappear while they conferred.

Just as the thought presented itself, in came another soldier. He had a broad face with a few fine lines around his eyes. He was probably in his mid thirties. He had neatly trimmed light brown hair and a matching beard. Something about his eyebrows screamed intuitive. He took in everything in a ridiculing kind of way. Like he was judging me harshly and didn't like what he saw. The high arch of his fine brows and the startled mien of his medium green eyes, unnerved me in an inconsequential way. I took note to not judge a book by its cover. He hadn't given me a reason to fear him yet. The strange combatant set his weapon and pack down, and spoke annoyingly slow in a British accent, "Ms. Marshall, I figured Banks told you about your predicament and who we are." His voice held an edge of derision.

I nodded but said nothing, so I could stew over how he knew my surname.

"My name is Corporal Bryant J. Toms and I'm the tech or mission intelligence for our team." I thought it was interesting how he told me his full name like proper name addresses were important to him. To me, he exuded more of a formal demeanor than the others. "As you may have gathered, our mission did not go well. The package that we must neutralize was not where it was supposed to be. We have to travel farther from here. So, we won't be going home anytime soon."

Toms paused to shake his head and then continued on, "We've decided that you have to come along. Either that or we kill you and bury your body so the locals won't know anything is amiss." I shuttered at his bluntness.

He noticed. "We just don't understand how you got here. Sub level two was not on the same level as the machine and us. The only thing that I could think of was that the radius of the anomaly stretched out farther than those arrogant scientists even knew."

Toms paused and looked down at his twisting filthy hands. "Oh well, no sense in contemplating all the particulars right now. Experimental science is not always exact. And time is not on our side. We're stuck with you and unless you can't keep up, then we'll be for awhile. Cross us and you're dead per Captain's orders. We're not your babysitters, nor your friend. Our Captain has decided that he will keep you under his thumb. So you will ride with him. I've served with him for several years now. He's a smart cookie and as good as they come. Judging by what he had to do on his tours in Afghanistan with the Jagers and what he's done on all our missions together these last few years, I know he won't hesitate to follow through with what he originally had planned for you. If you get my meaning, so be careful."

With that, I sunk down against the hard wall behind me as Toms walked out. Of course I would be a problem. I was not a soldier. I was a darn, dainty American business woman in a skirt and heels for Christ sake. I did still run somewhat as I did in track at school but how did that compare to this? And did I really believe we had traveled back in time? I always imagined that in the future, we could do things like that. Anything is possible. Did those scientists invent a time machine? And what kind of anomaly were they talking about? Was that why Stellar Solutions, who always built parts to space shuttles exclusively in facilities in the United States, had set up their business in the oddest of places like Israel? But why was there an anomaly in Israel? Maybe it's something related to the Earth's rotation and Israel's position within it. Oh Lord, I didn't know. I was not a scientist or a soldier. I needed to get back to office work. I had deadlines and a career that couldn't be put on hold. But if Toms was serious, would the Captain actually kill me?

I was still shaking my head and debating my choices, when Captain Eriksen appeared. I could tell he came from a long line of Vikings. He was intimidating. I never did business in Norway. As I was as petite as they came, I could tell it bothered him to grab my arm to lead me out. He grimaced slightly and loosened his death grip on my arm.

I accommodated the pull anyway, because if I was his traveling companion with a mark on my head, I'd better make it easier on him. I took these guys to be serious about what they were saying and what they were willing to do. On top of that, the sooner I got out of the room, the sooner I could figure out what was really going on.

He dragged me up a path that was more like a sacrificial plank. I had no idea what I was going to be dropped into. I slipped on a few rocks. My abductor easily caught me right before I fell. The ground was unsteady and my shoes didn't help. He turned those now cornflower blue, scolding eyes on me, and looked me up and down with a thoughtful expression. For the first time, his face betrayed him, and I could tell he may have a sweet side under that hulky exterior. Leaned down, he said, "Are you alright?"

"Yes, it's just these shoes."

"When we get to the closest town, we are going to remedy that. For now, I have a blanket up here in my pack for you to cover up with so you fit in somewhat."

"Fit in to what? What am I walking into?" I couldn't help but throw that back at him.

"Jerusalem. Back in the old days. Back before perfectly sculpted brown, hi-lighted hair, short skirts, and American sass," he said with a smirk in his funny accent. I took that as a compliment, but I was shocked all the same.

As we came up from out of where I was being kept, I started to think I may not be in Israel anymore. I didn't see any buildings or street lights. Nothing. It was eerily quiet. Eriksen picked up his pack and pulled out a blanket that he wrapped around my icy arms. I noticed Toms and Banks were looking over what may have been a map. Eriksen said nothing to me before headed their way.

The fourth soldier from the team came over and introduced himself as Sergeant Memon. He was the only native among the team. He had dark, thick hair and chocolate brown eyes with heavy lids. His almost square and middle eastern resembling face was accented with thick eyebrows and wide nose. Memon also stood the shortest of the four at about six or so inches taller than my five foot four-inch size. He was reserved but kind enough to acknowledge me. "Ms. Marshall, we'll be ready to head out in a few minutes. Do you have any questions?"

Well yeah! "So y'all are special services what?" I always drifted off in those military meetings I had to attend. Blah, blah ranks and such. I just waited on the guts or pertinent info to surface. Specifics about the military itself always appalled me. Hence the reason why I never filled out the CIA applications at my college's job fairs.

He grinned, "We are a Special Operations team called Task Force 28. Each of us were members of our native country's special operations teams that came together to form an elite team. I was in Pakistan's Black Storks, Eriksen from Norway's special ops unit called the Jagers, Banks over there, from the U.S. Navy SEAL team 4, and Toms from the British Special Air Services or SAS. We are basically retired from our country's military and are now contracted by companies from all over the world when private military needs arise."

"Sounds impressive."

He bent down to put something under his tunic into a strap on his leg. "What makes us so effective is we are a combination of each of our country's best skills, our experience, and our bilingual abilities. I speak Hebrew, German, as well as English. And it helps that we work good together."

Memon zipped up his pack. "These are my closest friends. The American took me awhile to warm up to being that he was a, as you Americans say, 'cowboy' and all." He smiled in a mischievous way this time. "But him and Eriksen go way back. They met each other during their time in Afghanistan working to control the uprisings and terrorist attempts there. Shortly after that, Toms and I came in."

Within a few minutes of waiting on the others, I got to know a lot about these men. Memon, who's age I couldn't ascertain, was not married. Nor was Banks. Toms was divorced after a tumultuous five years of marriage. But Eriksen was the mystery. All Memon would tell me was that he had a child that he never got to see. I inferred divorce from that and could honestly say I couldn't blame his ex-wife.

Memon's straight forward disposition made me want to believe what he and his team were saying. And everything I saw around me made me want to as well. The cave we climbed out of, the desolate landscape, the lack of light pollution revealing more stars than I had ever seen at night, and the seriousness of the soldiers' tones. They believed it, and in that moment, I couldn't believe that I could believe it too.

Out of the corner of my eye, one of their horses inched its way closer to me. He reminded me of a Spanish breed similar to a Galician horse because of his dark color and smaller size. The loyal animal already had a cavalry saddle and gear loaded on his back. I wondered where they got him. When the sweet horse pushed his head into my shoulder, the gentle act brought me the first wave of comfort that I had felt in the last several hours.

I pulled back my disarrayed dark brown hair into a cleaner pony tail to get it out of the way. Then, I reached up to pet the sweet horse like I used to when I got to ride horses at summer camp. Albeit those horses were probably tamer. That and the fact that I was wearing a skirt, told me it was not going to be an enjoyable ride.

I had to push that out of my mind and focus on being tough, so I didn't complain too much. Oh, that's right. That's what Eriksen was assuming would happen from an *American* girl. I planned to prove him wrong. And if we really did travel back in time, then women were also extremely reliant on men in this time. I needed these soldiers more than they needed to keep me around out of wanting to stay humane or for fear of a botched mission if someone found my body buried in that cave. I'd do what I needed to do.

The horse's black fur was warm to the touch. I found myself absolving all my immediate worries and leaning in to press my face against his head. The familiar smell of hay and sweat filled my senses. I closed my eyes and imagined I was back home in Mississippi as a young girl about to ride her first horse at camp. This subtle communication between me and this horse slowed my heart rate down and brought a small smile to my lips.

Maybe it could all be okay. I could follow them on their mission and then they would take me home. I could do it. I could do it and then I could get back home. And oh boy would Stellar Solutions hear from my attorney. I may never have to worry about a job again. But could I go back to my time? What if there were complications, and I died in the process. Steps made from shifting blades of grass and pebbles led me to instantly drop my smile. I opened my eyes to find a scowling Eriksen staring down at me.

Chapter 4

The trip to the closest town that the team called Ramallah was a six-mile trip and took us the rest of the night on our palfrey horses. I was falling asleep in and out on the way in an incredibly uncomfortable position but too tired to care. My head would bob slightly on Eriksen's chest and I would wake up, straighten up, and sigh when I realized the time travel expedition was not a dream. I pulled the blanket over me for the umpteenth time around my legs to cover the business skirt that was riding up to the tops of my thighs from sitting astride on the horse. I told Eriksen that I would only ride that way when he first lifted me up on the horse. He said something under his breath and swung up behind me. A man of a very little words. So why volunteer to watch me? Because he wanted to finish what he started back in the cave?

I shifted a bit because my rear was starting to hurt. I regretted it when I felt Eriksen's arm tighten around my chest. I felt like yelling, "I'm not going to fall off and slow y'all down! Get a grip!" But I didn't for sake of good relations. Yes, good relations. I knew all about that. It was my job after all. I had met some of the rudest people in my line of work and still had to get them leaving with a smile. I could handle one brute. When I said the word 'brute' in my mind was when it dawned on me, and I confronted Eriksen.

"That's how I know you," I said just barely above a whisper.

He heard me and countered, "How you know me?"

"Yea, you were one of the soldiers on the elevator at Stellar Solutions. You didn't look as malevolent then, with a baseball cap and your hair slicked back, as you do now. Wait a second, it was all of you wasn't it? The ones talking in German about me and thinking I didn't know what you were saying."

"Who knows? We do that often to women." I could tell the jerk said that with a smile. All it did was just fire me up.

I turned around and looked up to face him, "Oh I don't doubt it! Most women don't speak several languages fluently, do they?"

"No, you were the first to call us out on it."

"So that explains how you recognized me, but it doesn't explain how you knew my name."

At that Eriksen looked off and didn't say anymore. He just clenched his jaw and stared off into nothing. I took it that the conversation was over and I'd have to revisit it another day when we weren't so tired and cranky.

We got lucky though and made it to town before dawn, so the soldiers could sneak a 21st Century dressed woman into a room without anyone seeing. That wouldn't bode well. Especially not one similar to a drunken zombie stumbling into one of their rooms. When I found the bed and sat on it was when I finally took in my surroundings. Oh crud, it was the worst sleeping quarters I had ever been in. The small candle in the room and the moonlight coming through the four foot by four-foot window at the foot of the bed, lit the room just enough that I could make out a dirt floor, tiny and lumpy bed, and an old table beside me. It was depressing but quaint, so on that last thought, I figured it would do. I was just too tired from the traveling and the stress of my new reality to care. Without even trying to figure out how to go to the bathroom around the inn, I just dropped my head on the stale smelling pillow and passed plum out.

****

A soft breeze can bring the feeling of euphoria and joy when you wake up to it dancing over your face. Especially when you've gotten a much needed night of sleep. Or was it a daytime of sleep? That's right, I was in an old inn in. In the time of, I thought he said, 8 or 9 Anno Domini. And I had slept most of the day.

The claustrophobic room was just the way I remembered it from the night before, just not as much a medieval morgue as was my first impression. It had nice sunlight coming in through the window. Thank goodness for the breeze though. I would have never made it without air conditioning if it wasn't for the open window facing directly into the south breeze. I sat up and stretched just to realize I needed to pee something fierce. I swung my legs over the bed and reluctantly went to step on the dirty wood floor when I stepped on something that moved.

"Ouch, watch it!" said the strange voice of my mystery room companion. Over the edge of the bed, I made out that it was Eriksen who sat up from the floor rubbing his belly in a furious manner.

I dug my hands into my loose hair. "What are you doing here? Or down here for that matter?"

"Watching over you!" He stretched revealing big, well-toned arms.

"Oh what, so I need a babysitter in the same room with me now?" My voice wavered, and I cared not to hide it.

Eriksen raised one eyebrow. "Actually, the old man only had one room in his home available for guests. So it was either me or all the guys on this vacation, sweetie."

Hmm that sarcasm made me think he wasn't as much of a foreigner as I originally pegged him for. I paused with wide eyes, not sure what to say.

"And at least I let you have the bed," he said with a frown while still working to open his eyes.

I exhaled. Then, I bit my tongue when Eriksen rose from his make-shift bed. He wasn't wearing a shirt. My mouth went dry when I saw his broad, muscular textured chest, and sculptured shoulders. The moment scared me a little that I moved back to the other side of my bed. It was a little too intimate for me with this man I hardly knew.

He acted as if it didn't phase him as he walked over to the small table to grab his tan t-shirt that I presumed he's been wearing under his robe. As he slid his shirt over his head with his back toward me was when I saw the hand sized tattoo of the head of a ten-point buck of some sort on his right shoulder, another tattoo down his entire right arm with the writing, 'ANSIKTET FRYKT GODTA KRIGEN' which means something along the lines of 'Face your fear, accept your war', and two medium sized round scars below his left shoulder blade. It looked like the skin had been torn in such a gruesome way that evoked both empathy and repulsiveness. Putting it into context, I realized that those may be scars from bullet holes since he was a soldier and accustomed to dangerous missions.

Wow, that was a sight to see. Especially for my eyes. Not only because I had never been around or this close to real soldiers, but also because this fierce man chose to sleep on the floor instead of ousting me out of the bed. Or doing other things to me for that matter. I cringed on that thought.

As if reading my thoughts, he turned around with his eyes shimmering like he wanted to smile but hid it back. In the light, I could clearly take in his appearance. However powerfully built his frame was, he looked around my age with surprisingly calm, gentle, and deep set eyes. But man, they were some lustrous eyes. And the shape of his face was nicely proportioned too with a wide forehead and full lips under his beard, so even the slightest smile would be hard to see.

He ran his right hand over the top of his head which spiked up his short blonde mane more erratically than before. When his hand came back down to scratch his abdomen resembling deep thought, he shot me a glance that implied 'busted'.

I dropped my eyes right then in hopes that it wasn't too obvious. "I'm hungry," I said with a slight shake in my voice. I hated myself for it.

"I'll send you over some food. Stay in this room and don't go anywhere. I have to go get you some clothes." He reached for his boots. "Thankfully, you already have brown eyes. We won't have to hide your face too much for you to fit in without drawing attention as long as you keep your head down. Women of marrying age should not draw attention here." He paused and looked at me again for an uncomfortable few seconds and then started to leave.

With that, I jumped up, "Okay, so where is the toilet?"

Chapter 5

Hour after hour of sitting or pacing around the room, led me stir crazy. I didn't think it would take that long for him to find me clothes, and I assumed they brought plenty of money in preparation for potential problems on their mission. Me being their biggest yet. However, sitting in a tiny old room all day, using a pan to pee in, and dripping in sweat with no breeze to speak of made me wish I had the guts to stand up to them more.

Or did something go wrong? Were they figured out? Or did they leave me to continue the mission? If that was the case how long until they came back or would they at all? If I survived, Eriksen was going to get a piece of my mind. I was, as he pointed out, a modern day American woman. So I was accustomed to controlling more dominant, alpha type men than Eriksen in board rooms.

However, that was during a time when an education and pen were truly mightier than a sword or muscles. Sadly, education was pointless in this time, or was it? The door finally squeaked open during my devious planning to reveal the brute I had gotten reluctantly closer to.

"What took you so long?" I said before he was even through the door.

"Maneuvering through a first century town is not easy when you know your mannerisms and dress can send up red flags. Even our accents were tough to cover. We pretty much let Memon do the talking. Here, take this. It's not fancy, but it will cover your body and hair. These for your feet."

I jumped up, grabbed the garments, and smiled. In my hands, I held the ticket to get out of this room. "Thank you! Can I have some privacy?"

"Yeah, yeah sure. I'll step outside," I thought to myself duh, but he actually looked as if it took him off guard. I've got to remember that these men spend all their time with other men. They're not use to a woman as part of their team. Or at least as a tag along like me.

Pulling the dark blue robe over my body, I noticed its rough fabric scratch my skin as it hung loosely on my body like a trash bag. No curves showing, no originality, just plain threads to walk around a plain town. Joy! But at least I was getting out of this cellar that our host called a room.

The thin opaque black scarf covered my hair in a way that made me look homely and subservient. That clued that I was going to be treated second rate. My feminist side was screaming!

I went to open the heavy wooden door and saw that there wasn't a knob. All I saw was a small hole signaling a lever that opened the door. I pushed and found Erikson standing there with his hands on the railing facing a way from me. When I first met him in the elevator days ago, I never imagined him like this. He was so serious and stern now. He rarely smiled and scared me half the time. He was nothing like the guy who chuckled with his friends like a school boy that day. I made a point to remember him similar to how I first met him, so I could handle the man on a mission version of him.

I brushed by him and frowned when he grabbed my arm. He effortlessly spun me around to face him, "Wait! There are some things we need to go over first. No talking to anyone. You may be able to speak their language but your accent is too risky. Trust me these people know the difference and women did not speak much in public in these times. Just the men. Also, their way of talking is all they've ever known besides the Romans coming around here every now and then. Your personality, slang, and accent will stick out like a sore thumb. Even your flawless skin and the way you carry yourself is not typical here. And pay close attention to your veil. Don't let it fall off. God only knows we can't afford you exposing those damn salon highlights. They're subtle enough but could be an unwanted distraction. Women were very plain in these times. We have to be careful. With that being said, two hours is the max amount of time around town so you can get fresh air. That is it! There are a few hours left in this day and we need to be back in the room before dark. Got it?"

Keeping my mouth shut while I allowed him to finish his power trip, left me angry. I defiantly looked back at him. "I'm not a kid. I've worked in and around many different nations. I know how to be careful with different cultures and customs. It will be fine." I turned on my heels and started to head down the rickety stairs of the house when the front door opened, and I immediately recognized Banks.

With a smile I acknowledged the younger soldier, "Banks, how are you?"

Banks glanced passed me at Eriksen and then back at me, "I'm great Ms. Marshall, but try not to smile. Women here don't usually smile in public at men."

"Oh, my bad." I walked up to him and grabbed his arm so he would escort me much to his surprise. As we walked, I talked low but prodded for answers. "So where is the mission taking us?"

"Talking to the people around here we gathered that Parker, our rogue scientist, has passed through here."

"What is Parker up to?"

Banks shut his eyes and then looked back at Eriksen following behind us. "He carries a virus."

"A virus? Is that it?"

"Any virus that these people have not been exposed to is bad. Without the proper medicine, immunity, or resources, the common cold could wipe out this and many surrounding towns."

"So what is the virus?"

"Maybe Ebola. We're not for sure what he took or how much."

"What? We barely handle Ebola in our time."

"Sshhh... Keep it down," Banks hissed at me as he led me by the small of my back out outside. I noticed the sun was lower on the west and the sky ochre. I didn't have much time to sight see. As I stewed over his words, I took in the scenery. Banks pointed to his left. "Over there are aristocracy and priesthood constructed homes. See how they overlook the Temple Mount ahead?" The buildings weren't huge but were well built with buttressed passageways between them.

Banks continued, "Over to our right is Jerusalem's version of a forum".

I asked, "Latin for public place outdoors, right?"

He nodded. We walked a few hundred feet until the market place was all around us. On both sides, booths lined the road side by side filled with lively activity. Dust was everywhere, but I could make out other women's faces hidden under their hoods all looking to the ground as they passed. I immediately did the same to continue to fit in with their ways.

Every now and again, I glanced up to see booths with ripe vegetables and fruits. Textiles and other commodities were on display in an unorganized manner, but it didn't stop customers from diving in and making purchases.

Men seemed to pay more attention to Banks which bothered me on some level. I guess it was the idea that I was walking second fiddle to a man. I simmered out of it when I realized it gave me more chances to look up at the hustling all around me. I took it all in. With all the commotion of people back and forth, I still didn't feel suffocated in the town center like I would in a modern day parade with this many people. I couldn't figure out why it was more relaxing but that maybe it was because there were no cars, huge signs, or kids running around everywhere. The kids I saw were perfectly behaved following along with their moms.

One kid caught my eye when I noticed he was staring at me. His mom was struggling to carry her basket of goods when it slipped from her hands and splattered all the contents over the dirt road. I stepped away from Banks to pick up some of her goods for her. She smiled at me and in the Aramaic language of the Jews said, "Merci" meaning "Thank you".

"You are welcome. I'm Kyla," I told her speaking in my best Aramaic as well but minimizing my dialogue to just what was needed.

"I'm Dulce and these are my children Paul, Michael, and Sarah." The little boy that was originally staring at me was Paul, and he looked no older than eight. Michael had to be around six and Sarah around four. All had dark, wavy hair and big brown eyes.

It was neat to meet people from the past so much so that I forgot how risky it was until Eriksen stepped in to save me, "Mistress, where is your husband?" His voice stern and with perfect Aramaic, to my surprise.

"He died last year," she said remorsefully and adjusted the light brown veil that had slipped to the crown of her head.

"You are by yourself raising these three children?" This time Eriksen sounded tender in his questioning.

"Yes, but we manage just fine."

"Why don't we help you get your things back to your domus? It's the least we can do for a widow and her children," Eriksen told her. I was so taken with Eriksen's kindness. It was refreshing.

When we got to Dulce's small home outside of town, she offered us some of the wine and cheese that she just purchased. Eriksen declined, but Banks wasted no time accepting the offer. He whispered to me that networking was vital in espionage. "The more they talk, the more we can learn," he said. Banks had been a formidable interrogator on missions. To me he was a nice young soldier. I could tell that to everyone else, he could be intimidating.

I didn't mind that my last hour would be spent at this woman's home. It made me feel good seeing the look on her face when her guests decided to stay and visit. I admired her ornamental plants scattered around and her nicely organized triclinium.

Dulce looked older than me or Toms even. But she told us she married at sixteen and was married for eight years when her husband died. She wasn't all that pretty and her smile though sweet, was crooked. But she had something lovely about her in its simplicity. Maybe it was the way her wavy hair caressed her shoulders gently like a slow, flowing stream. Or the perfect arches of her brows setting off a nice heart shaped, olive face. She had the same brown eyes as her kids and a longer nose like my Jewish family had. I paused to look at it again when I discovered that feature was similar to mine.

Could my family have come from her and her kids or her extended family? I shook off the thought and looked around for Eriksen noticing that he stayed outside the door. I inferred that he may have stayed outside on the street to make it not too imposing. Dulce didn't bother asking why or how we were all related, she just seemed glad for the company.

The sweet young woman poured some dark red wine from an ornamental carafe made out of limestone pottery into two small wooden cups for me and Banks. I took a tentative sip allowing it to linger on my tongue. It wasn't real sweet. It was smooth with a burst of some kind of berry trailing at the end. For a rudimentary wine, it tasted pretty good.

Banks conversed with Dulce and I let my mind drift again but this time back to her kids. They peeked around the curtain from their room every few minutes to gather their own intel. I just smiled at them and wondered again about this virus Banks told me about. Is it already unleashed? What would it do to these kids? My heart started to speed up and my mouth instantly became dry. I didn't know if it was the wine or anxiety from knowing what was going down. And what this mission was all about. I guess I started to panic and told Dulce to excuse me as I briskly ambled out the door for fresh air.

When I got outside, the breeze instantly cooled my sweaty face. I dropped down to squat and put my head between my knees. A soothing voice came from behind, and I recognized that it was Eriksen. "Are you okay?" he asked.

"Yes, I'm fine. Just got a little dizzy from the wine."

He sat down next to me but kept his eyes forward. "Yeah, wine will do that."

"Banks told me about Parker and the virus."

"Oh?" He scratched his cheek and kept his eyes forward.

"This doesn't even seem real. Why did 'Stellar Solutions' allow this?" I asked.

"I don't know about their motives, just the mission and info pertaining to that. All companies lie anyway."

Getting a little bolder I asked, "You have a child?"

He turned to me and frowned, "Who told you that?"

"Memon."

"My team needs to learn to keep their mouth shut." He paused. "I do have a boy, Aiden. I don't get to see him much." He didn't elaborate. He just picked up a small pebble and tossed it down in front of us with a pinched expression across his face.

I squeezed my eyes shut. "I'm sorry, I'm just taking this all in and those kids in there may end up right in the middle of this nightmare."

"We're all in the middle of it. Every future generation will be affected. Especially your ancestors. Aren't you part Jewish?"

As my panic attack subsided with the assistance of our banter, a sudden coldness hit my core. "My father was part Jewish and practiced that faith, my mother is more of an American mutt. She is a mix of Indian, Irish, and Italian." I pressed on. "She is also a Catholic. I remember that had been a source of contention between them before the divorce. Him practicing Judaism and her practicing Catholicism." Why did I feel comfortable enough to share my life story with Eriksen?

It helped when he decided to do so too. "My family is Catholic, but I haven't been practicing it lately." He ceased speaking to look up and down the small walkway between Dulce's home and the town. "But what blows my mind right now is that in about five or so years, the birth of my faith will begin." He scratched his cheek again, and his awareness of what lied ahead wasn't lost on me.

"Yea, that's right. The prophet, Jesus."

"Jews believe he was just a prophet. Catholics believe he was the son of God."

"What do you believe, non-practicing Catholic?" I asked bluntly.

But he just smiled at me. Not a big smile, but enough that I relaxed back into the conversation.

"Practicing or not, I believe he was who he said he was." The massive soldier sitting next to me now had a gleam of pride in his eyes.

But with that shivers ran down my back at what he said. It was a lot to take in. Not only were we on the trail of a potential mass murderer, but he was threatening to do it around one of the most pivotal times in human history. Was that coincidental?

I looked over at this man calmly sitting next to me staring ahead. He had his hands clasped together on his lap and his long, thick legs were stretched out. I took in the blunt angle of his jaw under his scruffy beard, his elements' weathered face, and the Adam's apple bobbing in his throat. I also noticed something shiny below his neck laying on top of the visible chest hair just above the closure on his garment. Why didn't I notice it before that moment? "What is that, a necklace? Your dog tags?"

He grinned, "Na, we had to leave behind our tags." He reached into his robe and pulled the silver chain out. "I guess you got me. It's a crucifix."

****

Walking back to our accommodations, gave me time to process a few things. As we passed more little ones, I stewed on Eriksen's words and the new revelations that he revealed to me about himself. It wasn't the first time I was in the company of someone who seemed religious even though he tried to deny it. However, it was the first time I met a cold-blooded killer who wore a charm with the depiction of a holy man carved into the metal. Another contradiction in regard to Eriksen that I kind of admired but didn't know how to take.

Banks walked beside me on the way back and didn't say much either. All of us seemed to be in deep thought. When Banks finally spoke, I listened. "We are leaving in the middle of the night and need to get some quick shut eye."

"I don't know how much sleep you poor guys are getting in a barn on piles of hay," I mused.

"Thanks for the concern, but we're good." He smiled for just a second.

"So, why so early?"

"We learned that a traveling caravan came through a few days ago on its way to Macedonia, and Parker was most likely on it based on what the townspeople told us. Parker was dressed in the proper B.C. garb, but he must have stood out like a sore thumb being all in a rush. Dulce even remembered him. Therefore, we've gathered that Parker's target is not the Jews here in Jerusalem but possibly the Roman Empire. Macedonia was an important hub for the Romans in this time. Similar to how New York is for America. If the virus starts there then it could spread more at an alarming rate around the entire empire, including Ramallah with Dulce and her kids."

"Geez," was all I could say. But they were including me in their plans for a change. I held on to every word he said. However, the weight of the responsibility we were given started to sink in. I could tell the team originally didn't think it would be this complicated when they signed up. What was aggravating was that they were told by the company that only four could travel back in time. I'm still not sure how I could, but I cursed fate because these men could have used another real soldier instead of me.

The group had decided that we needed to leave a few hours after dusk, so we would be able to travel inconspicuously through the open terrain. I cringed at the thought of another trip through the night but Banks reminded me that if we met too strong of an opposing force and had to use modern force, we would. However, their weapons were extremely different than the Roman soldiers' weapons. Combat with weaponry was the worst thing that could happen, but they would use them if needed. Each man had a MK 16 with a ten-inch barrel and silencer tucked inside blanket rolls and tied to the back of the horse, a side-arm under their robe, and a few knives stashed here and there on their bodies.

Eriksen, the sniper of the team, carried his prized .300 Win Mag secured on his back and under his robe during travel. According to Banks, he took great care of that thing. I hated guns, but tried not to show it as he spoke. He went on to tell me that if it came to any of them needing a gun, every step needed to be taken to remove the bullets, cut up the gun shot wounds from the bodies so it looked to resemble more of a sword wound, bury the body deep in the Earth, and finish off anyone who saw the act.

I looked up at Banks with what I could only imagine was horror written all over my face. He turned to me. "Don't worry. It shouldn't come to that."

I studied him more as he kept his eyes ahead. No matter what he said, I wasn't afraid of him. I didn't know if it was because he was from America like me and we had that in common, or if it was because of his young face and dimpled smile. He smiled a lot at me and I couldn't help but smile back even though he was a Texan, I wouldn't hold that against him. And as the rest of the team, save Toms who remained extremely suspicious of me, finally started talking to me more, I started to feel included.

****

That night, we headed out as soon as dusk hit. The traveling north at night seemed somewhat relaxing even with my back up against Eriksen's chest the whole time. The air outside was a little chilly during the ride, but my riding partner blocked most of it with his body heat. We didn't talk anymore about our lives back in the twenty-first century. He was back to his usual reserved self. I could tell he was extra cautious about our surroundings because every now and again he would signal to the others to stop for a few minutes so he could listen.

Eriksen kept his right arm tight against my chest. I guess to make sure I didn't fall if I dozed off. It was a tender gesture, so I caught myself wondering what he was like as a husband, father, or even a lover. He didn't strike me as the type that could leave his job on the field per se. But the one moment I feigned to look up at him when we were stopped, I caught him looking down at me. He had a slack expression on his usually austere face. Caring almost. Maybe he didn't decide to kill me, because he couldn't bring himself to hurt a woman. Even though I knew these men had probably killed several women between all of them either accidentally or as part of their missions. I started to finally doubt that I was in any danger from any of them anymore.

When the sun finally showed its first rays, the temperature rose fairly quickly. Besides the sounds of the horses, I could hear the wind pick up over the land. It was a peaceful sound, but I couldn't shake that it was foreshadowing something terrible. Within a few hours, we came upon a broken wagon and a man crying.

The elderly man kept pointing further north but was not saying why. Eriksen allowed us to stop long enough to check on him. He was a squatty, old man with a grey beard and robust belly. If it wasn't for his dark skin, I would have pegged him for a Santa Claus. He was cut up pretty good on his face on down to his hands. And there were a few dead victims scattered around him. My insides quivered and my shaky hand caught Eriksen's attention. He grasped my hands firmly after taking me off the horse. Then, he ordered me to stay back.

I watched from the corner of my eye as Banks took out some medical supplies from his first aid kit in an incognito way to keep it hidden from the old man. Memon followed to address the man as Banks began patching his cuts up. The old man's name was Viggo. He was a Roman citizen from the town of Tripoli who was on his way back from trading in Tyre. Viggo and his wife were ambushed by thieves who left him for dead, took his goods, and his wife. He pointed around at two dead bodies saying those were his slaves that were slaughtered.

I was close enough that I could make out the Latin language Viggo was speaking to Memon, the team's primary interpreter. Banks continued to bandage him up. Toms was off to our left keeping a lookout. When Eriksen motioned for us to leave without offering any more help, I spoke up for the first time in eight hours.

"Eriksen, we've got to help him," I said as he passed me heading back to our horse.

Eriksen immediately turned & scowled at me. "No. We don't."

My hair lifted on the back of my neck. "So, you're just going to walk away?"

"No. I'm going to ride away."

I frowned. "Not funny."

"Kyla, things like this happened often to these people in this time. We have no obligation to anyone here, just the mission."

"You're a pain in the...!"

"Excuse me?" He bared his teeth, albeit, they were nice straight teeth. Then, he stepped up close to me.

"Um." I drew a breath and looked back over at Viggo. He wasn't paying attention to our exchange back and forth. He just sat there with his hands in the air.

"What did you just call me?" Eriksen hissed at me bringing my attention back to the one hovering over me with a vehement intensity. His jaw clenched as I wavered.

Trying to avoid his gaze, I pointed to Viggo. "It looks like he's praying for help. Possibly to your God, right?"

"He's Roman, he has several Gods. Now let's go."

I grabbed the massive soldier's arm. "What if he could help us?" My diplomatic skills started to kick in. "If he is a Roman citizen, he could help us get around."

Eriksen looked at my hand on his arm. "He'll slow us down."

Toms, who was following our discussion behind Eriksen, came to my defense. It was surprising. "Captain, can I have a word?" Both walked a few steps away and tried to keep their voices down low. I strained to hear but caught a bit of the tail end of it. Toms looked up at me before addressing Eriksen again. "She has a point. This mission is getting more and more complicated, so we do need all the help we can get. He can ride with me."

After a few seconds and more words exchanged, I could tell Eriksen had conceded. However, while still out of ear shot of Viggo, the man had the nerve to discuss with me again the rules regarding conversations with people of this time. "Even though, you know the language, you don't talk unless absolutely necessary. Neither will I nor Toms & Banks, just Memon. Also, we're keeping to our story that we are men hired by your father to protect you on your way from your home in Hebron to our destination in Antioch where your brother resides. Got it?"

"Yes sir," I said while grinding my teeth. I knew my cheeks were red. And as his eyes were shooting darts into mine, I shrugged and averted my eyes back to Viggo just to shake the tension. Remind me not to get into negotiations with a military man again. I won, but it wasn't easy. Next time I won't be so lucky.

Memon strolled over to speak with Viggo and told him of our plans. Viggo clasped Memon's shoulders with an appreciative gesture before fixing his copper colored mantle more securely over his grey hair. Then, after helping Viggo gather his essentials and bury the dead, we were off again. We traveled for most of the day through the valley. Every now and then the men would dismount and look around at the ground looking for hooved tracks. If something was found, we would continue on but in a fast trot following the horse tracks.

Finally, by mid day, we came upon movement ahead, and I could make out the outlines of four men carrying something big laying over the back of one of their horses. Eriksen raised his fist signaling for everyone to stop.

Within seconds, Viggo and I were ushered off our horses and left behind as the soldiers rushed off ahead. I watched as our men charged the convoy without fear or delay. I grabbed Viggo's rough hand and noticed his pensive expression grow even more weary. I squinted to see the fray better and saw that Eriksen had already pulled his first opponent off their horse and jerked his head in an unusual way that left the body dropping limply down to the ground. Memon was in hand to hand combat on the ground with another, and I shrieked when he took a hit that threw him to the unforgiving earth. He jumped back on his feet flawlessly like a gymnast and swung his fist back with ease knocking the other man cold out. My heart unclenched suddenly with pride at the beauty in the soldiers' movements. Each taking out their opponents with little resistance. It was amazing how well trained they were.

I could tell Viggo was just as astonished. He removed his hand from mine and drew it to his chest. "By the gods, they did that without swords. Like Spartans of old," he said in his language while looking ahead. As I was advised, I did not speak, just smiled while he continued. "Where did they come from? Are they Roman soldiers in one of our legions?" When I didn't answer, he just looked back and suddenly his eyes glowed. "They have her. It is her, and she's alive."

He took off running toward our heroes and my heart was full. It was his wife. She rode with a huge smile in front of Eriksen. When they came close enough, Eriksen let her down. She ran into the old man's arms. Her grey hair was down and long to her waist. It flowed all around him when he took her into his arms. I ran up, and she pulled away from him to thank me as well. She smiled with her huge green eyes shimmering with tears. She had crow's feet around her eyes and fine lines around her dainty mouth. Her skin had been protected from the sun quite often, and her composure showed to be classier than anyone I had met so far in that time. I could tell she was from money or maybe protected politically. She took my hand and introduced herself as Aida. The incredible moment took me away so much that I responded back in her language, "I'm Kyla. Are you hurt?"

"No. No, I'm well. Thank you, Ky Lah. That is a name I've not heard before."

"Oh, no. Just Kyla. One word."

"Oh, well my husband and I are in your debt. You and your family saved my life." She took my hands and smiled down at me. "Are these brave men your brothers?"

"No, they were hired by my father to take me onto Antioch to retrieve something from and see my brother."

"Well, you are most certainly blessed by the gods to have such capable men in your company." She was breathless and shaken up a bit but still very complementary.

"Yes, I am," I said and could tell even I was blushing. Viggo took her by the hand and led her back to the soldiers who came up wearing a scratch or two. I could tell they looked nervous about what transpired as they continued to look around in hopes that no one else had seen the encounter. Eriksen advised everyone that we needed to keep moving. If the villains had friends, then it wouldn't be long until we would be met with more force. Force that would mean more than hand to hand combat. Memon came back with one of the dead's horses and Viggo and his wife mounted without question. Quickly, we were on the move again. This time we moved parallel but off the beaten path for coverage.

Aida and Viggo spoke back and forth for hours on the horse next to us while Eriksen continued on the journey silently behind me. When we first got underway, he was breathing hard from the violent encounter and his body was radiating an excessive amount of heat. His big, calloused hands clenched tightly around the reins and shook as if they were still battling. I resisted the urge to cover them with my own to steady the adrenaline still coursing through his body. Truth be known, adrenaline was still pumping through mine.

What would happen to me if they had lost? I took a deep breath and reluctantly laid my head back upon his chest to stabilize my own emotions. I'd never been close to anything like that fight before in my entire life. When my body relaxed against him, he shuddered and took a deep breath. I froze and relaxed further into him when I realized he wasn't going to curse me or push me away.

Eriksen had a light smoke smell, from something he ate earlier, overshadowed by a masculine sweaty scent made obvious from the dampness protruding into my back. I could feel his heartbeat racing faster and faster as I took note of the beats. The thumping of his heart steadied mine as I slipped into slumber thinking of these men moving in unison in battle with their cold, steady gazes and strong, flexing arms pulling me to safety while I gave into their comforting protection.

Chapter 6

I awoke to the sound of a stream where we stopped at to give the horses a break. My traveling partner, whom didn't say a single word to me, dismounted and helped me down off the horse. Viggo and Aida disappeared behind the shrubbery to the stream for some water with Memon and the horses. I tried my best not to make eye contact with Eriksen while we waited.

When Viggo, Aida, and Memon came back, Eriksen and the rest of the men headed down with their horses. I stood in my same spot staring at their backs as they disappeared thinking of how thirsty I was. No one acknowledged me, so I just turned around and stared off into the distance. A few minutes later, Eriksen showed up and moved toward me with his eyes downcast. "You have ten minutes. Relieve yourself, drink, and come right back. Got it?"

I nodded and walked by everyone else coming back in from the stream without casting a look their way either. When I went through the bushes and saw the stream, my knees went weak. It was so beautiful and so inviting. I rushed down and washed my face. I cupped some water for a cool sip of the shimmering fresh liquid. Instantly, I felt better and the tension dissipated. No one was anywhere close or could see me at all. They left me to my own devices to give me privacy. A whole ten minutes of it. Wildly, I started stripping off the heavy blue tattered dress and shoes. Then without thinking, I pulled off my undergarments and ran into the stream until it covered my shoulders.

I hadn't swum in anything but a chlorinated pool in years. The lake in Illinois with my mom was like this. I was an only child so we took vacations with my aunt and cousins. My older cousin, Jake would always torment me to jump off the high cliff and I'd do it just to prove that I could. Jake and I were close. I was missing him and his kids something fierce. The bushes crunched for a split second, but nothing was there. Just the breeze whipping the pine needles around the trees. My lips began trembling and my eyes dashed wildly around the bank. I wiped my face with my hand and slowly made my way up to the river's edge. Without a second to lose, I hurried to my clothes. Rushing to throw the old garment over my head, I saw someone coming at me from out of the corner of my eye. I let out the breath I was holding. It was just Banks. But did he see me naked?

"Hey, I was just coming to check on you," he said with a wry smile.

"I'm okay. I still had a few minutes, right?" I asked agitated.

"Yeah. Sit. Let's relax before we've gotta get going again." He patted the sand next to where he now sat.

"Sure." I sat on the bank next to him. Then, I pulled my hair over my shoulder to hopefully hide the frizziness of it, so I at least looked a little decent. I didn't know why it mattered.

We sat there for a minute or so looking at the stream before he finally spoke. "I served in Iraq for two years."

"You did?"

"Yeah, I saw and did some pretty bad things."

I kept quiet prompting him to continue. He seemed more serious than I had ever seen him and that was odd for him. He had his knees pulled up and his elbows laying over them to where I could take in his hands. They were rough looking and had callouses in key places that said gun shooter. He rubbed them slightly but didn't pay attention to me staring. "Being here makes me feel like it was worlds away. Like it never happened. Another life, you know?" He spoke slowly with that strong Texas drawl.

"I guess, I wouldn't know."

He continued like I wasn't even there. "The rush feels good though."

"Rush, what do you mean?" I said keeping my eyes steady on the man. He had this vacant stare. He wasn't looking at anything, just off. Off into nowhere. It made my blood turn cold. I had to remind myself that it was the friendly, fellow American, Banks sitting next to me. He seemed like a stranger suddenly.

"Fighting. You begin to miss it after awhile. Taking a life. No fear, just reaction. But it takes me back to that hell. Those people in Iraq didn't care about anything, kids, women, nothing, just their plight."

I shivered as he continued, "These men here, you know the ones from earlier? They reminded me of those beasts in Iraq. That evil. We took those lives today like they were nothing. They didn't stand a chance. But they were evil weren't they?"

At that, he looked at me and his usually open face was tight and gaunt. I didn't know what to say. But it still didn't look like he was looking directly at me. His brown eyes were so distant. I sucked in my lips out of nervousness and looked off to avoid the fact that he was actually scaring me. I noticed he continued to stare at me, but I kept watching the dancing bugs above the water and the light flickering down into its depths. Maybe he just needed comfort. Maybe he wasn't looking at me at all. It was strange.

And even though Banks was friendly most of the time, I realized his dark side must want out every now and again. He's a good guy so why so troubled. I felt sorry for him but didn't know what to say. Still with him strangely staring at me, I didn't know what to do either.

There was a movement to my right, and I tilted my head up toward the sunlight to see Eriksen approaching through the bushes with cold, hard eyes on Banks. He addressed me but kept his attention on Banks. "Time to go. Head up to the horses."

I said nothing but jumped up and brushed passed him. When I made it to the bushes, I heard Eriksen addressing Banks with a deep, harsh tone. I stopped to look back and saw them both toe to toe in an argument taking place just barely over whispering levels. I couldn't imagine what they were going back and forth about, but the posturing between them made it evident that Eriksen was scolding him for something. When Eriksen turned and noticed me watching, I blushed and dropped my eyes to the ground. Then, I backed up right into Memon. Memon grabbed my arm and pulled me out of the shrubs back toward the horses. "Had a good break?"

"Not much of one. I was disturbed," I said with a smirk.

"Oh yes, by Banks, huh?"

"Yeah and the other pain in the rear."

Memon stopped and turned to look at me with those thick eyebrows squeezed together. "You don't know much about soldiers, do you?"

"Never been around y'all, no."

"Do you realize what a skirmish like what we got into earlier does to us?" he asked while leaning in toward me.

"No, I know it made me feel sick." The sound of my heart beats thrashed in my ears at the memory.

"Good. That is a normal reaction. For soldiers who have done it for several years, non-stop, it does a lot of different things. Sick isn't how we react anymore."

"Oh, how does it make you feel?"

"For some, excited. For others, horny." He said and smiled.

I dropped my eyes in hopes that he didn't notice me cringe.

"And for others nothing. It's like we are playing a game with no consequences. But that is when it gets scary." He paused. "In truth, for all of us, it's a struggle whether we want to admit it or not. Some more than others. Banks and Eriksen go way back. Eriksen is like a big brother to him. You know, Banks had a hard time after his last tour before joining us. In fact, he scared his girlfriend one night, and she called the police."

"What did he do to her?" I asked as I analyzed his words against what I already knew about the kind and friendly Banks. It couldn't be him.

He shook his head and scuffed his boot on the grass. "That is something you'll have to ask Banks one day. But I will tell you that your government overworks their soldiers, so it's common. They are left on too long of tours or even non-stop ones. The constant battling, gun fights and daily fear, desensitizes them to where they can no longer function in normal society. Banks isn't even as bad as hundreds of your other soldiers, trust me or he wouldn't have made the team. But being here in this time with how high the stakes are, surely is having an effect on him. It is with me."

"Eriksen seems to be handling it okay."

"Okay? I wouldn't say that. He just hides it better. Eriksen has his demons too. I know I shouldn't say too much, but you probably should know us better being that we're all stuck together."

I lifted my eyebrows to urge him to continue.

"Eriksen and I were on a mission in Africa that went bad. I won't divulge too much, but I will say he still gets nightmares often from it. His faith is the only thing that gets him through from day to day." He looked to the bushes to make sure it was still clear. "We all have our war baggage, Kyla. You're still safe with us, I promise. I just thought you should know."

I noticed the clouds covering the sun in a ghostly way and thought about the tall Norwegian and his intense blue eyes. Besides being brash, he did hide his past trauma well. I felt sorry for him for the first time since knowing him and still felt there was so much more to learn. "Well, why was Eriksen so mad at Banks?" I asked.

Memon shook his head, looked back at the bushes, then looked back at me with a smile that didn't quit reach his eyes. "Women. You are oblivious, aren't you? Banks didn't watch you swim just to sit with you and talk."

****

Toms made a small fire as we all stretched our legs and backs on our next stop later in the day. Even though the men wanted to continue on, Aida was still hurting physically from the abduction. Viggo's leg, that had been slashed, needed another bandage and Aida was complaining of nausea. The sun had not fully set, but the men decided a few hours of rest was a good idea for everyone before we made the last push through the night. Memon was sentry this time and took his place a few feet away against a large pine tree where he ate a packaged granola bar from his rations to help keep him awake.

Banks tended to Viggo and didn't say much else to me. He supplied the couple with a blanket that they took rest on. Toms sat up against a tree trunk slipping off to sleep, and Eriksen disappeared into the woods looking for more sticks to keep the fire going. My fingers kept twirling my hair and my mind was racing. I couldn't sleep yet. So I decided to walk to further stretch my legs.

In the trees, I could hear the squawking of a sparrow and see the insects scurrying to prepare for the end of the day. It was nice and peaceful. I was still stewing over how much Banks bothered me at the stream. I didn't like how his intentions were not my own.

I picked up a beige rock that was covered in green spots. It was cool to the touch and very pretty. I stood there admiring it when I heard a voice. "You know; you should be getting some rest." I jumped. A few feet from me was Eriksen sitting up against a tree with his rifle partly taken apart and spread out neatly on his blue blanket.

I stuttered my words to him, "I needed to get some... I just couldn't rest... yet."

He was applying an oil based solution to specific places on the rifle and rubbing it in with a small cloth. The intensity in his eyes was gone now almost like he enjoyed the trivial task he was performing.

"What are you doing?" I asked.

"Cleaning my guns. Come sit, and I'll show you."

"I don't like guns."

He dubiously regarded me. "To each his own. But tell me, if you were being attacked by someone who wanted to hurt you, and they were as big as me, what would you do?"

"Scream, run."

"What if they caught you and bound your mouth?"

"I don't know." Trying not to seem flippant, I moved to sit next to him. "I carry mace."

He laughed and I saw how nice it was when he finally smiled. "I guess that would work but this..." He picked up his side-arm pistol to show me. "...it will guarantee that you will get away. And you don't have to get overly close to your attacker to neutralize them. Have you ever shot one?"

"No. I was going to try years back but when I had a client dealing with blowback from a deadly shooting, I lost interest. I still see the dead family and the carnage that shooting left behind." My hands trembled on my lap, and I looked away to avoid his gaze. It was a tender moment for me. I felt a warm touch on my left hand and met his sympathetic and understanding blue eyes. "Ever since I worked for that client, it has been like that."

"What happened?"

"They had a mass shooting next door to one of their facilities in France. I still remember the faces on the dead family of four that were killed. They had no way to defend themselves. They were like fish in a fish bowl in that small theatre. The little girl in the picture was tucked under her momma in a way to hide her face. I cried after reviewing those pictures. Four doses of Prozac and three days later, I PRed that event without a problem. Job well done, but I never took a case from a gun client again."

He nodded. "Yea, I can understand seeing bad things and how hard letting go is. It takes bravery."

I was about to ask him to elaborate but thought better of it. But to break the quiet, I got curious. "So, who taught you how to shoot?"

"My father. He was a military man too. He died of cancer a few years back," Eriksen said softly and withdrew his warm hand.

"I'm sorry. That must have been hard."

"No, he was a jerk."

"Really?"

"Actually, just hard on me. Expected a lot of me. We would fight when I didn't do something just right. There was this time when I was fourteen and was hanging out in the barn with some friends. We discovered my dad's private stash of Akevitt." He saw my confusion. "It is a popular liquor back home."

I nodded.

"We thought it would be cool to partake of the old man's liquor and surprisingly got in the mood to rearrange the barn after. Maybe move Annie, my sister's Fjord horse to the same stall with one of our male horses." He paused to recollect more. "Needless to say, I got in much trouble." Eriksen's accent really surfaced when he spoke freely.

"What happened to you?"

"Besides being beat and grounded? I was also forced to clean his Case tractor with a toothbrush while I was going through the worse hang over of my life." He swiped over his face with his right hand remembering back. "Then, to make it even worse, when I got finished I thought I could go in and sleep the rest off. Nope. He woke me up complaining that I missed a spot on the left front tire and made me go out to finish the job with my hands."

I grimaced at how hard just cleaning a big tractor would be and then to add being nauseous to the mix. "You turned out okay. I imagine he's proud." A compliment, but I meant it. And I really liked how he started opening up to me.

Eriksen picked up another piece of his rifle to clean. "The funny thing is, I cried when he died." I hid my shock, and he continued, "I hadn't talked to him in years before his passing but cried anyway. He used to always say 'A man can cry, but it better be for a really good reason'." He just looked ahead.

I thought I could ask him some more about his dad, but refrained. He seemed so vulnerable in that moment. Eriksen continued, "I guess I can't blame him now. His way of dealing with the effects of war was that he'd come home a jerk and drink all the time. My way is to shut everyone out no matter how much counseling. You asked about my son. I just didn't know how to be the man she needed and the father he needed." His remorseful eyes turned on me. "Not after everything I've done and seen."

I shifted on the ground. "Well at least your dad stayed around..." was all I said. And then quickly moved to change the sensitive ground we stumbled on. "Okay, so show me."

"What?"

"Show me how to shoot."

He cleared his throat and smiled. "Are you sure? I thought you didn't like guns."

I played with my nails debating that same thing. "I don't. I just feel like in this time and in this place, you are right. It is a good thing to know. You know, if anything happens to you guys. I've got to survive, right?"

He nodded and picked back up his smaller firearm. "Okay... well this is a Beretta M9. It is easy to use in combat and for personal defense. I have a silencer on it, so we can shoot a few."

He stood up as if glad for the reprieve too, and I followed suit. Shoving his tunic up to his elbows exposing his strong forearms, he held up the gun. His right hand was positioned over the trigger and his left hand came around the bottom with those fingers curling around his right fingers. Stretching out his arms with a slight bend in his elbows, he pointed the gun toward a pine cone on the ground further ahead. "Step back just a bit."

"Okay". *Pop, pop, pop***.** It was unnerving how the pinecones flew up into the air. He continued shooting in a way synonymous with letting off some steam, and I stood there watching. His gaze ahead was firm, and he tightened his bottom lip just a hint between shots. The strength in his solid forearms revealed long line of tendons reacting to each pull of the trigger. No matter how much I hated guns, deep down on some basal level, I liked to watch him shoot.

"Ready?" he asked.

My mouth gaped open. "I guess."

He came up behind me, and I felt his warm breath tickle the back of my neck. "Okay, hold the gun in your right hand like this." I reached my arms out and tried to imitate his original position as much as possible while he helped. "Don't put your finger on the trigger until you are ready to commit, got it?"

"Got it." A bead of sweat ran down my forehead.

He held my hands in place and spoke low into my right ear. "Aim at one of the pine cones where you can see the target through the sights right here. See those three dots?"

"Yes, Okay."

Eriksen nudged my feet apart with his right foot. I took a breath trying not to show I'd gotten uncomfortable. "You need a wider stance," he said hoarsely.

"Okay," I said and more sweat trickled down my face.

"Are you ready?"

"Yes."

"Take a deep breath to steady your shot and..." He reached around me and clicked the safety off. "...when you're ready, shoot. I'm right here."

Pop... The gun kicked up just a bit to where I missed the target. More determined, I squeezed the muscles in my arms and the gun tighter. *pop, pop, pop.*

"You got it!"

I lowered the gun, and he grabbed it from me. "Whoa, got to put the safety back on when you stop."

I turned toward him smiling from the rush of excitement pulsing through my veins. "That was different!"

He smiled with a sparkle in his eyes and proceeded to yank back the slide to clear the remaining bullets from the chamber. "Not bad for your first gun practice. Now, we clean it."

****

Tripoli at early dawn is a neat sight to see with the Roman architecture appearing out of the darkness. We went from small whitewashed cracked stucco homes to magnificently tall concrete columns on all the buildings. Fired clay brick walls and copper colored tiles adorned the roofs. Arches and domes accented important spaces, and sculptured trees and hedges outlined the terraces. Or maybe it was because I've never seen Roman buildings in real life.

The porter at Viggo and Aida's villa escorted us into a semi-extravagant domus. It was ornate with columns wrapped in green vines, black stone flooring, a huge fountain in the center of the foyer, and tall, dark wooden doors that led to lush gardens. I couldn't believe the ambiance of this 1st century home. Aida was so kind to put me in a beautiful bedroom that exuded immense opulence with its huge bed, in-room tub, and rich velvety curtains leading out to a private balcony. I was in Heaven. And on top of it, I didn't have to share it with anyone.

After the servants brought me up warm water, I bathed for over an hour in a wooden tub made out of a giant oak barrel and lined with tin. The luxurious feeling water was sprinkled with rosemary and lavender. Simple but amazing. Several days of traveling across the countryside would do that to you.

A plate of blackened chicken with lentils was brought up later, and I devoured it. I then emptied the goblet of wine from the salver and took in Viggo's terraced gardens. Standing on the balcony in my state of relaxation, I saw men down below conversing. One with dirty blonde hair that must have been Eriksen and the other, Viggo.

Turning back inside, I collapsed on the woolen mattressed bed thinking about Eriksen, the snippet into his childhood. It was nice. But I didn't like the orders Eriksen laid on me the moment we arrived in Tripoli. He told me I was going to have to stay with Viggo and his wife until they were finished with their mission. I didn't know what to think of that, but I knew I'd enjoy being with Aida in this delightful home.

And then Eriksen's smile came back to mind. My thoughts bounced back and forth until I realized I just couldn't sleep yet. And would I want to? I am in an ancient Roman city! Though it was mid-afternoon now with night approaching, I still had enough time to see some cool things. I dressed back in traveling attire and snuck out the room.

The townspeople were actively packing up their booths and scurrying to their homes. For a predominately Roman town, everyone was so dirty. Maybe I thought that because I had just had a bath, but I expected more cleanliness from Rome's citizens.

Next, I strolled into the forum into a much bigger crowd. Everything from fish to pottery was being cleaned out as coins exchanged hands and merchants reassessed their inventory. The heat bouncing off the ground and the close quarters of people all around in this area, was making me miserable. The few women I saw that were left in the market, did not have their hair covered. I gingerly removed my scarf too, so I could feel the cool air on my head. It made a huge difference.

There were two russet stallions approaching with their owners roughly leading them. And dung was present many places along the stone built road. Keeping my eyes down in hopes of not making a misstep, I ran into a solid structure. I stepped back and took in a man several inches taller than me dressed in a grey tunic that was belted at the waist and stopped at the knees revealing dirty legs and sandaled feet. "I'm sorry," I said in my best Latin and tried to maneuver around him.

He grabbed my arm, and I noticed his strength as well. "You are a pretty little thing. What is your rush?"

"I've got a few more things to buy before dark. Please remove your hand!" I said with a sternness that was rather typical for me when I got mad.

"Hmm. I'd hate to keep you from your perusal of Rome's treasures. Let me help you."

Another man walked up beside me with one brow raised at his friends' catch. They both towered me in such an ominous way that my heart started to speed up. There were two Roman soldiers off to my left keeping watch of the activities all around. I was about to yell out when the first man pulled me back against his chest and put his grimy hand over my mouth.

Within seconds, I was pulled into an alley way, and I freaked. Screaming and kicking, just made the second man laugh. "Now, quiet down. You chose to be a courtesan. I'm in need of service."

I kicked him in the best place I knew that could bring a big man down, which caused him to release me. But for just a second. It must be an age old move, because he did not act surprised from it. He bounced back without delay. Tearing back at me, he yanked my hair while the other man continued to laugh. "Guards!! Help!!!" was all I could get out before the bigger one threw me to the ground and collapsed his weight on top of me.

"Yell all you want pretty one, we *are* Roman guards. Just off duty right now. They won't do anything to us." His hand went around my neck to pin me down and terror blinded my courage. I stared up at the darkening sky wondering how I got in this horrific nightmare. Tears rolled from my eyes and down my cheeks. His hair soaked in sweat dripped onto my face and I could smell his musky presence all over my body.

As he pulled my hands up above my head with just one of his hands and shoved them into the ground, my knuckles scraped the rocky earth. I could feel him tugging at his clothes, and I let my sanity drift as the tragedy continued to unfold.

Thunk. My eyes popped open to find his friend falling to the ground. My attacker ceased his advances on me to look back. Before I could take it in, the weight that was suffocating me retreated, and I rolled over to finally take in a full breath. Standing a few feet away from me was that evil man facing another and forming a fighting stance. He moved forward at a quick pace and pounded into the unknown man's chest knocking him smooth to the ground.

Working to stand and run, my legs shook uncontrollably so badly that I collapsed back onto the hard surface beneath me. A sound of intense impact resonated in my ears as I saw my mystery savior kick the monster in the face surprisingly from his spot on the ground. The shock was making it all blurry, but I noticed my hero jump on top of his fallen opponent and pound his fist in to him over and over again. Blood was beginning to cover the losing man's face, but the man on top just continued to throttle him uncontrollably.

"What goes there?" An older voice yelled from down the way.

The massacre stopped and bloody hands reached to pull me up. I slapped at them and tried to gain the strength to run. He picked me up cradling me in his arms and ran with me until we were far enough from the scene. I ceased resisting him and laid my head onto his chest. He had a familiar scent. A citrus and metallic smell that I recognized to be Eriksen. When he stopped to set me down outside the town, the darkness was all around. Even in the dark, I could see his slanted brows as he moved my hair to check my neck, hands, and arms. "Are you alright?"

I couldn't yet speak. I just shivered and stared off.

"He didn't..."

"No!" I got out and another tear raced down my cheek.

"You're in shock. Give me your hands." He took my hands in his to warm them and pulled my head down to his chest. "It's over. I'm here."

Chapter 7

My room didn't have the same glow and excitement as before, but I was still thankful to be back in that sanctuary. Eriksen didn't ask me any more questions or berate me for my ignorance as we headed back to Viggo's villa. He asked if I needed anything and left me as Aida cared for me. I wanted to ask him to stay or even to not leave Tripoli without me like he was originally planning, but I decided it better not to show too much weakness. It was stupid what I did. A lack of sense. I should have known that a woman traipsing around an unknown town without a man, was ill-advised. I just didn't realize how different this time was from my own until now. As Aida brushed at my hair and spoke kind words, a rage battled deep inside my soul.

Conflict and hate go hand in hand. I was accustomed to them, especially now. Not so much with wars, but with my own emotional battles from my childhood to the present. However, there were good days. Days when I could recollect happiness but couldn't fully remember why. Like when I was lying in bed with the sun brushing the panels of my aunt's curtains ever so gently that I could see all the fragments of the air swirling in a dance of elation and tenderness. I just remember smiling and nothing more. These were the times of my younger years in Northern Mississippi. The smoldering South along the great Mississippi River, an area rich in war history.

I grew up playing on the battle fields there masking in the thoughts of the men of whom died in my nation's Civil War. Tall structures marking the places where they fought and rested. The North and the South camping and resting sometimes within ear shot of each other. I remember thinking how stupid it all was. I was a child with distinct theories on adult behavior like any other child. We thought they were all stupid including our ancestors. To combat during the day when the sun was above but talk to each other when the sun disappeared like they were all friends again. What a paradox.

What fools I always thought. Men and their wars. Well, I grew up learning that there was a lot more to these wars. But no matter how much history I studied at Ole Miss, I still thought wars were all the same from the beginning of our time here on Earth till now. Man groups together in order to protect themselves. An alpha and charismatic leader emerges from the group to guide them. Before long, the clan grows and grows until they decide they need more resources to survive and eventually collide with another clan or tribe. It all ends the same. Someone suffers at someone's benefit. And raging wars off the battlefield, sadly go the same way. From my emotionally battered past to the new trauma that was unfolding in my psyche, battles were no stranger to me. And maybe I needed to compartmentalize all of it the same way.

I guess it was the simplest way to look at life. But was anything about humans and tragedy ever that simple? I went to sleep in Aida's care thinking of Eriksen physically saving me but hoping for emotional strength.

****

An air of excitement blew through the villa. Aida rushed into my room with servants in tow just as the sun was coming up. She was giddy like a school girl talking on and on about her incoming visitors. Apparently, her cousin was a Roman Senator, by the name of Nicator, and he had been invited to come to dinner upon his arrival in Tripoli. Tripoli was not Aida's hometown. She moved with Viggo there from her birthplace in Perusia, Italy when she was first married.

I sat up listening to her tell me about her family as her servant, Leta, yanked at my hair and brought dress after dress to my face to check the color against my skin tone. As Aida went on and on, my mind drifted. A Roman Senator was going to be here in my presence and I wasn't allowed to talk per Eriksen. Then, I paled thinking about my friends. "Aida, did my men leave yet?"

"Oh no, they are still here. Since you seemed to be doing better these last few days, they were finally planning on heading out this morning onto Antioch, but Viggo convinced them to stay."

"How, why?"

"I think we know more than you think we do young lady. Firstly, I don't think your father could hire men like that for you unless you were on a very important expedition, or unless he was extremely rich. Which leads to the second reason, there is no way those men are just fishermen. Fishermen don't fight the way your men do. Viggo and I don't fully know who you are or where you come from, but we do know you need our help." She touched the green satin on one dress and frowned with disapproval.

She continued, "Viggo wants to do more for you than just offer you a place to rest. He wants to help you in your plight. We won't ask questions that you don't want to give answers to, but we beg you to trust us to help where we can. And one way that we can help you in whatever you are looking for is to introduce all of you to my cousin. He is a powerful Senator, Kyla. And because you saved me, his dear baby cousin, he will do all in his power to help you. Your friend, Eriksen, agreed and they are all getting ready to help us receive my cousin within the hour. Please, take your time getting ready. Leta here, will help you."

The slight young woman bowed sweetly before me wearing a pale blue dress in her hands similar to the blue of her own dress just a little fancier than hers. Leta was most certainly of Egyptian descent. She was lovely with her dark brown, curly hair pulled up behind her head, small eyes of sadness, full lips showing a wide smile, and dark brown skin. I could tell her and Aida adored each other though. There was a connection between them like mother and child, and I smiled inside at them both.

Aida made her way to the rustic door. "I'm glad you are back to feeling better. Dinner today will be wonderful entertainment for you and me."

When she walked out, Leta smiled again, "You are the most beautiful woman I have ever seen. And I always thought my Aida was the most beautiful. It will be a privilege to work to make you presentable to our guests."

I laughed taken aback by her comment. "Oh, no I'm not anything, trust me. But I thank you still." That beauty she spoke of made me a target just a few nights back. I shuttered as the memory drifted across my now rested brain. However, with each day, my emotions started to become more steady. I was beginning to feel like my old self. Even more so when I found out my friends hadn't left me. I was ready to get out and make myself useful, the hell from a few nights ago be damned.

"I have never seen such perfect, porcelain skin in any Roman or Jewish, as they claim you are. Your beautifully arched brows. And your teeth! How did you get them so white and perfectly straight?" Leta stopped bashfully, "I'm sorry, I don't usually speak so freely, but I've never seen anything like you."

"Well, thank you Leta. You have made my day."

"Made your day? How does someone make a day?"

"Oh, never mind. Let me see that dress you have there."

"Well it is made of the finest silk from the Persians and the blue will surely show off your skin and big, light brown eyes."

I stood while she dressed me in the softest fabric I had ever felt. I felt like a different person altogether, royalty almost. The dress hugged me perfectly around my breasts showing creamy white curves that I had never shown before. I always dressed modestly in business blouses that covered all the way up to my collar bones. I had never worn anything as feminine and nice as this. The bottom of the bodice gathered tightly around my small waist then flowed so elegantly down to my little feet. There were several layers in the skirt that made the dress shimmer when I moved.

I peered into the small mirror and almost didn't recognize myself. The dress was just so feminine. It matched my skin tone nicely and my caramel face framing hi-lights, the salon did just a few weeks ago. I noticed the extended stay lip color, I wore when I worked late, was still hanging on to my lips giving me the needed 'pop' to contrast the pale colors. Gotta thank Cover Girl Mauvulous for that. I never got much attention when I was in the states. But apparently, I was a looker in Rome. And the dress really piled on the vavavoom.

Leta continued with her ministrations and pulled up my long locks into a pile on my head leaving a few caramel strands dancing down my face. "Beautiful," she said as if she was proud of her work. "Just beautiful. The daughter of Venus, you are."

I shyly looked away willing her to stop. Too many compliments were again making me nervous. I didn't know how to take it. "Thank you."

"So, which of those men that you are traveling with have your heart, daughter of Venus?"

"What? Oh, no, it's not like that. They are just watching over me for my father. He's entrusted me with them."

"Hmm, well you must be blind then. Let me be frank if I may, that tall bear of a man with the shining blue eyes is beautiful, that he is."

"Who, Eriksen?"

"Oh yes, he's brawny with a body like Achilles. He keeps his eye on you."

"What do you mean?"

"You don't pay much attention to him do you, foolish girl? But he's always watching you."

"No, not Eriksen. He abhors me, trust me. He's just doing his job as protector." Did I really believe he saved me for the sake of the mission?

"I disagree, but it is you that will lose out when he turns his attention to another Roman goddess." Leta whirled around and grabbed the other dresses on her way out. She stopped at the door with a questioning look on her face. "But what I don't get, if you don't mind me asking my lady, why do they all look so sad? You know, the men with you? So sad and angry? Even centurions in the Roman army smile from time to time." I bet they did. I had no love for them right now, obviously.

I wasn't sure how to respond to her, so I gave the most honest answer I could think of. "Maybe they have seen a far more amount of death than Roman soldiers." And my answer rang truer than any reply I could have given her. My tough band of brothers had seen a lot. Not just one battle, but many in their short careers.

"Hmm, maybe. They just have that look that you see on a man who's been imprisoned in a dungeon for years. Very disturbing." And at that, she turned and left leaving me to my thoughts again. My men were having trouble fitting in. How could I remedy that? Or even more importantly, why was I viewing them as my men? This was getting strange. But why wouldn't I feel like we all belong together? Heck, they were the closest connection I had to my family and home. And I was just recently saved from hell by one of them like the big brother I never had.

After I messed with my dress for a few more minutes in hopes of covering my chest better, I heard a knock at the door. "Please come in."

In walked Aida all dressed up nicely in a crème colored dress cut similar to mine. She took me by the arm and escorted me down the long hall. "I'm so glad you can join me and leave that room for a change. These dinners are what I look forward to the most, and I get to share it with a close friend now." I smiled at her feelings toward me and walked with a happy stride to enjoy the party too.

"I can't believe it is almost dinnertime. I will be frank, I thought I'd never see my husband, my home, or even get to entertain ever again. You made this all possible for me again. I'm still so thankful. The gods brought you to us."

"I guess that could be so, but we were just traveling the same path. That's all. Anyone would have helped." But no one else helped me in that alley but my own people. I pushed back the resentment again.

"Do you know how traveled that path is?" She waved at a young man sitting at a bench who blushed at the attention. His eyes like a hawk unwavering on us.

"No, not really."

"Rarely traveled. In fact, that is why Viggo told me it would be safe to travel it with him and our servants. I never travel with him. He just had to bring me along this time and swore we'd be safe. They killed our servants without mercy and took me, leaving Viggo helpless in wonder for my safety. He was so distraught. Both him and I have been having horrific dreams because of it. Do you think it gets any easier?"

"Easier? You mean dealing with the trauma of the event?"

"Yes."

"I don't know yet. This is the closest I've ever come to something like that. But those that I've known, that have experienced it, say it takes years of counseling before they can at least cope with it. They never forget, though."

"Counseling? Maybe you can be my counsel and me yours. If that is what a counselor does. You are already special to me and will always be my guest until you decide to leave."

"Will do, Aida. Will do," I said with a smile and we walked on.

****

Loud baritone male voices echoed from the east side of the villa. Sounds of laughter and jubilee permeated from inside the walls of the dining room. The tall door opened to a grander room than I imagined. Inside, it had a long wooden table that had the Amish craftsmanship beat easily. There were at least sixteen place settings lit with romantic candles and silver plates paired with thin, delicate glasses.

Aida led the way and as we entered, all the men at the table stood immediately. The instant silence was unnerving. I had walked into meetings already in progress before and never felt this odd. All twenty male eyes were on me, and I didn't recognize any of them right off. Aida guided me to a chair that Viggo pulled out for me.

As I sat down, Viggo introduced me to the man two seats down on my right as everyone else sat to continue on chatting. He looked close to Aida's age and had a disturbing gleam in his eye. His gray hair was cut short and judging by the robe he was wearing; I could tell he was the Senator before I was told his name. "Kyla, this is Senator Gaius Calvisius Nicator. Senator Nicator, this is our guest, Kyla Marshall."

"Marshall, huh?" said the Senator as he chewed on some pork. He didn't bother waiting to finish before he spoke again. "I've never heard of that surname. Where do you hail from?"

"Hebron, sir," I said bashfully. Why am I acting like this? "Control the boardroom, Kyla," is what Walter use to tell me. "All men or not, if you don't have them in the palm of your hand, they won't believe you have the situation under control." He'd be so disappointed. I knew I had to get a grip. However, Tripoli's atmosphere, with their unaccustomed and violent ways, was so intimidating.

"Ah, but you are too beautiful for a Jew with a surprisingly pale complexion. And I've never heard of a Jew named Marshall. But then again the Jews always surprise me." He laughed, took my hand, and kissed my knuckles.

Out of the corner of my eye, I saw a man sitting next to Viggo across the table, shift in his seat. I smiled at the Senator and turned my eyes to the movement. It was Eriksen sitting taller than all the other men at the table with his blonde hair brushed back and his piercing blue eyes staring straight at me, which strangely comforted me. He was cleaned up nicely and wore a golden trimmed robe with just enough arm length to hide his tattoo. His jaw twitched, and I gave him a small smile to say hello without drawing too much attention. He swallowed hard and turned his attention to another at the table.

The moment of freedom gave me a chance to gaze around at the other occupants at the table. I noticed Banks and Toms next dressed similarly handsomely but did not see Memon. They smiled gently at me and calmed my nerves considerably too. There were a few other unknown men down the table and one in particular on my right, closer to the Senator, that I didn't right off recognize either. Strangely, I got the feeling while looking at this man's mannerisms, that I did know him. But how?

Senator Nicator drew my attention back to himself and introduced the man in question next to me as Cyrus, his new consultant. "Mistress Kyla and my dearest Aida, you must try the fine wine I brought in from Bethany. Locals say the Dead Sea's salty vapors help grow the best grapes."

"Yes, thank you." As I picked up the glass, I noticed Eriksen tense up, but I ignored it. I needed the wine. I ignorantly soaked up the moment and took a sip of the sweet red wine. The herbaceous tasting liquid had a touch of willow bark and honey. It was good in an after-dinner dessert kind of way. I continued drinking. The conversations went on around me. Senator Nicator directing most of his questions to Eriksen. I imagined it was because Eriksen was the leader of our group. His questions were of wonder on how Eriksen looked very much like someone from Germania and how a fisherman could fight so well. Eriksen denied it, but I could tell the Senator and his counselor still had their suspicions.

Finally, the Senator moved his attention back to me and eyed me from head to toe with delight. "So Mistress Kyla, I see you are not married but why? You are well passed the prime age of marriage. Are you a widow?"

I gave him my best smile. A little wry, but it had to do. "No, sir. I just haven't had the opportunity."

"Well, maybe more opportunities will present themselves here in our lovely Roman town."

"I wouldn't be so sure." And with the attention back on me and the wine working amazingly fast, I confidently drifted into business mode in an attempt to help with the mission. And I felt invigorated from it for the first time in days. "So, Senator how goes the Empire these days?"

"Oh, fine just fine. Under our great Imperator Caesar Augustus, Rome is flourishing with our endeavors beginning to reach as far as Magna Germania now. Did you know we have begun building a fortified trading site and settlement along the Lahn river in Germania?"

"No, I didn't realize."

"His excellency attributes this idea partly to his wife, Livia, or third wife for that matter. She feels good connections with the Germanic people will help further our goals of assimilation and dwindling of their barbaric nature, you?" He licked the vegetable sauce off his forefinger, and I winced.

"I do too believe in furthering relations with others but doing it in a way that doesn't lead to animosity among the conquered."

"Conquered? I like the way you talk." He looked up to Viggo. "Viggo, you have found a rare Jew on your travels, haven't you?"

"Yes, I have," Viggo responded.

The Senator turned back toward me. "So Kyla, may I call you that?"

"Yes, sir." My eyes drifted to Eriksen who gave me a warning glance.

"How would you better relations, as you say, with these barbarians? I would love to hear a woman's perspective."

"Well if you want to show them the greatness that is Rome, then actually show them. Invite some of their tribal leaders to Rome and entertain them with lavish meals, shows, and worthy trade. When they feel they are valued and are somewhat important to Rome, then they will feel more eager to become a part of your culture. You see Senator, the study of mankind has always shown that if men feel inferior to other men, they will continue to fight against the opposition in order to prove their relevance. Everyone wants to feel their ways or their civilization is important in the greater scheme of things. Annihilating it without permission will never work. Resentment will always fester and wait until the right time to strike back when provoked."

The Senator paused for a moment and I began to think I misspoke. My extensive negotiating experience, as well as my studies in international cultures, history, and human interactions, got the better of me. Basically, I talked without caring. Who could blame me? The way Rome handled its conquests, was barbaric. And then they acted so nonchalant about it.

The Senator looked around at all the guests before turning back to me. "She is clever, this one. Was it your father that educated you in the ways of man and business? I must meet him. Hmm, no matter." He picked up a few grapes and tossed them into his snobby pimpled face. "I can't decide if the words you speak disturb me or enlighten me. You do speak well and with good Latin for a Jew. Interesting, just interesting. And the shows that you are referring to, are they the gladiator games? And what of this high value trade? That is all perplexing, woman."

His companion Cyrus, spoke for the first time all night. "What is perplexing is how this lowly status female understands the complexity of expansion and war. As if changing one thing in negotiations truly effects the outcome or dominos."

"Dominos? I have no idea what you mean, Cyrus. What are these dominos?" asked the Senator.

"Senator, it is a game of ancient times. But you see she thinks the smallest positive gesture will avert the progress we've had with the Germanic people. I agree as you do too, Kyla. Basically if you change one thing in the way we deal with them, it will have an effect on everything else that follows. The question is, will it be positive or negative for Rome?" Cyrus said with his grey, crude eyes focused on me. He was talking in circles; I couldn't figure out why.

Then, the Senator turned to Aida, who was clearing her throat in a way to move along the conversation. "My dear cousin you must partake of the dessert made especially for you tonight. They are raspberry hazelnut truffles."

"Oh yes, cousin. I have been looking forward to trying them," he replied. The cousins began to talk back and forth about her savage ordeal on the road between Tyre and Tripoli.

Me, on the other hand, finished my third glass of wine. Or was it my fourth? With the wait staff constantly refilling our glasses, it was hard to measure my alcohol consumption tonight.

Cyrus leaned over and whispered something to the Senator during the Senator's conversation with one of his associates. With glassy eyes, I smiled at Eriksen timidly while Aida giggled toward me. I didn't remember much about the rest of the dinner, but that it had a second amazing dessert that was lost on me. When it was all over, I observed Eriksen approach me and lift me from my seat. He gave Banks a look and thanked our hosts while he guided me out of the dining room.

When we entered the hall out of ear shot of our hosts, he stopped and swung me up against the wall. "You're drunk!" Was the first thing in several days that he said to me since my almost serious assault. I didn't think I could have bounced back like I did if the violent act was allowed to be completed.

I replied, "No, I'm not. But what does it matter? I'm not on the mission anymore anyway, remember? Apparently, you are very happy to be leaving me behind." It felt good to get out my frustration about the decision he made regarding me on our arrival here.

"You are so naive."

"Naive. What does it matter that I'm drinking?"

"Cause you'll give a way who you really are. As you Americans say, 'Loose lips sink ships', Kyla."

"I didn't say anything to give us away, and I won't while you're gone either. And the only thing that I could possibly give away is that I'm a highly educated woman in a man's world. They could not comprehend time travel even if they stumbled upon it themselves. Really Eriksen? Come on, have faith in me."

He laughed ironically and rubbed his hand over the back of his head. "Just be careful." I was surprised he didn't bring up my carelessness in the forum. Trying to drop it from my own mind, I held back the 'thank you' I should have given him for rescuing me and beating those men within inches of their lives. "And we're not going anywhere too far from here now. The mission is here."

"What do you mean? Parker is here in Tripoli?"

At that, he grabbed my arm and steered me down the hall. My feet worked overtime to keep up with his long legged strides. The man handling was oddly not disturbing from him. When we got to the gardens and close to a bench, he sat me down and paced in front of me.

The night air was cool to my intoxicated face. The red flush I was wearing on my cheeks from the drink must have faded as I leaned back and tilted my head up to feel the light breeze. No sounds were made but maybe from the occasional locust as it rubbed its file and scraper together in a harmoniously act making organic music in such a peaceful way.

I looked up at Eriksen waiting for his response. I found myself looking at him as a *man*, not my keeper. It's the first time I had done that since I had known him. I couldn't deny how much of a risk he took to save me. Me, the original flaw in his mission. Or the fact that he shared with me an intimate moment from his life several days ago. Or that I shared one myself with him.

Through hazy eyes, I really studied him. I could make out his looming gaze. The similar expression he had after he saved me from the alley. I then admired the sexy Adam's apple bobbing in his throat, his tall stature as he paced back and forth while rubbing the back of his neck. Oh, but then I saw his full mouth twitch under his growing beard. I shook my head to keep my mind straight but it didn't work.

As he continued to struggle with what he was dealing with, I noticed those crisp blue eyes look over my head to watch the entrance to the gardens with caution. Then, he moved his eyes over my entire body with slight hesitation. I averted my gaze off him when his eyes met mine. I didn't know what got into me; I had looked at those same features for days. But this soldier, with his serious and deadly demeanor, started to seem alluring to me. It must have been the wine.

It was suddenly warm outside. I was blushing all the way up to the tops of my ears. I turned my face in hopes that he didn't notice. But when I looked up again; he was still watching me. The look in his eyes brought me back to the day at the stream when he and Banks argued about me. Maybe he *did* desire me. Did he scold Banks because he wanted me?

With a little new found bravery from the wine, I decided to test that theory. I stepped up and put my hands on his solid chest and felt his heart rate speed up. This stoic soldier took one step back and tilted his head. Then, he slowly wrapped unsure arms around me. I couldn't help it, I made what I thought were doe-eyes, lifted up to tip toes, and stared up farther into his eyes. He was water, and I was thirsty tonight.

In a husky voice he asked, "What are you doing?"

"I don't know. What are you doing?"

"Looking at you."

"Why? Why have you been looking at me? Always looking at me," I said in a coy way.

"I ... I don't know. I guess I have been. Just trying to keep you safe." He paused and cleared his throat with a cough.

"Is that the only reason?"

Then, he touched my cheek with gentle fingertips. I froze because I couldn't believe it. They brushed along my jawline and across my collar bone. But then he pushed away from me and faced out toward the garden.

"What's wrong?" I asked timidly.

"Wouldn't it be nice? That for just a moment, we could pretend to not care about what happens to these people or to our time? This mission has gotten way more complicated than we planned. Desperate men, on a ship stranded in the middle of the ocean, have mutinied in situations similar to this. I trust my men and their conviction, but I know it's getting tough. It feels like the weight of the world is on my shoulders." He turned back to me looking me up and down. "And then here you are."

"What about me?"

"I don't know." He paused with a blank stare. And the more I studied him, the more I admired the man in front of me. "I guess that maybe you give me hope."

I smiled one of those smiles girls do when they realize the guy before them is struggling with his words around a girl. "How do I give you hope?"

"You're here." He looked down at the ground and spoke next choosing his words carefully. "Just when I think we failed because of what happened in Jerusalem, I start to think of you. How you showed up. And I wondered if that was a coincidence, but I don't believe in coincidences."

He shook his head and made a funny face at me. "You know in Greek mythology, there is a reference to a Phoenix. A bird that is said to be reborn out of the ashes of defeat. Like a new hope. Christians refer to it as a symbol of renewal."

"I don't follow. I'm nothing special. And to be frank, I showed up before your failed first mission." Just had to throw that in now that the wine was still talking.

"I don't know yet. I have three men in that house that need orders on what to do next. In our time, it is typical to think fast when new plans are needed. But the parameters and dynamics were so different than what we have here. Then, I see you acting like everything is going to be fine. Even after..." He stopped before finishing to restate. "You know, having a good time like you Americans always do. And I feel that maybe everything is going to work out after all."

He twitched his eyes as if holding back a smile, but I smiled for him, "It will be okay, just do what you do best and what your training prepared you for. These people of this time are lacking the knowledge and expertise that you have. You got this, big boy." As soon as the words left my mouth, I blushed again.

With that he did smile and seemed to relax for just a second. And in that moment, I was actually starting to know him. More than I had known any man before. I stewed over that thought and the fact that he had kept watch over me since the moment I showed up. My heart sank, and I didn't know how to react to him staring at me while my mind processed what my heart already knew.

He broke his gaze and reached out his hand. "You need to go to bed, so I can meet with my team, understand?"

"O...kay." I stepped up hesitantly and let him lead me out of the gardens, down the halls, and to my room with no more words between us. He opened the door to my room, ushered me in, and slowly followed me until I turned around.

"Get some rest." He turned toward the door to leave, took two more steps, and stopped with his hands clenching in and out of fists. Was he struggling with something? I partly wished it was because of me. His shoulders tensed, and I noticed the fresh wound on the back of his neck from his confrontation on my behalf. However, he didn't look back at me. He just stared down at his feet. "Whatever happens Kyla, you'll be safe here now." And with that, he walked out.

Chapter 8

Small talk with Aida was tiring being that my mind was on Eriksen almost every day. I couldn't believe he was having an affect on me. Every time someone walked down the hall, I looked up in hopes that it was that tall Norwegian with his crystal blue eyes. She advised me that they were fine. They were asked to accompany the Senator to a neighboring town to speak with a representative of the Roman army. Knowing Eriksen, he was probably just going along to get more intel before he decided how to proceed.

It had been several nights since we talked in the gardens before he left. I had thought of him until I fell asleep that night hoping he would come back to my room. His mind was on the mission, but my mind was on him. Him? That big ole brute with no personality? He was the polar opposite of what I was always attracted to. Why was I fighting my attraction to him? Why did I not like the idea of needing a man? But the more I thought about him the more I recognized that I did care for him. And I became aware of what I actually liked about him too. The odd idiosyncrasies that made him, him. I liked the way he was so particular about things being so inerrant and precise. His silverware at dinner had to be laid back down in its proper place at the right angle to his plate. His weapon laid out perfectly when he cleaned it before he taught me to shoot. Or the way he measured Jerusalem to the next town making sure the map key was accurate that first night. His quirkiness was bordering on OCD, but it was surprisingly fun to watch.

His uncomfortable demeanor when he dealt with my flirting the night we met Aida's cousin, was so sweet. He tried to remain so decent and gentlemanly with me. It was so astoundingly out of character for him. That was not how I imagined a soldier would act. Banks with his cursing, Toms with his spitting, and Memon with his twitching all were a stark contrast to Eriksen's impregnable composure. Which was under fire that moon-beamed night in the gardens because of a certain someone. I blushed just thinking about how I acted with such a hardened soldier who fought the good fight and didn't take advantage of my drunken state. Were all Norwegian males like that? I didn't know, but I was growing to love contradictions.

Sitting in my room, going out for walks in the gardens, and eating three square meals a day was getting boring. I needed something to do while I waited on the team. Time was moving way too slow causing me to worry. Worry about the men and the possibility of never getting back home. And I needed to clear my mind of Eriksen before I got too attached. I knew a little about gardening from watching my grandmother, so I spent some time helping in Aida's gardens. Horticulture in Southern Europe was not too different from Mississippi. When I walked into the courtyard, my eyes took in the space and how it was laid out beautifully in a peristyle fashion. Four huge columns surrounded a veranda of lush green plants and brightly colored flowers. There was a small, round pond in the middle with stone half walls all around it.

I wanted to find the berry trees Eriksen and I sat close to last night. I wanted to know more about them and whether they were edible. They reminded me of blackberries back home that I use to scavenge off the vines in grandma's backyard. As I was strolling through on the first work day, a young woman approached me wearing a plain tan dress and dark hair that was pulled back in a low bun. She had a mousy look about her with thin lips and small eyes. She stood somewhat taller than me with long arms and legs but was proportionate and graceful. "Good day. My name is Julia Ligarius."

"Hello Julia, I'm Kyla."

"Kyla? I've never heard that name before." We started to stroll through some pear trees with low growing branches that I touched gently as we talked.

"I get that a lot. It's more popular where I am from."

"Ah..., well I tend the gardens as well as help in the kitchens. This part of the garden is my favorite." Her prideful smile obviously hid the sad look in her eyes.

I looked away to keep from asking. There were at least a hundred feet of colorful plants planted one after the other. The Tower of Bells plant bloomed a beautiful violet flower with a dark, almost black, center. Contrasting against those cool violet colors were the Corn Poppies in bright red as well as a huge patch of spirited rouge Anemones. The white flowers that were intertwined between all the arrangements were done so in a way that felt pure to the eye. It was all so inviting and magical.

"I can see why, Julia. Listen, I would like to help with the gardens. I have been known to have a black thumb in the past, but I am a quick study."

"Black thumb?" she inquired.

"Yes, opposite of green thumb."

"Oh."

I knew she didn't get it, so I changed the subject. "Julia, I am looking for a berry that I noticed the other night. It grows on a tree which is quite different from the berries I've encountered."

"Oh yes, that is a morus plant."

"Morus?"

"Yes, some call it a mulberry. Come I'll show you." And she led me to the exact plants I was inquiring about. "See, they have a bumpy texture and a sweet taste. Taste one." She removed one of the two inch berries off the tree, but it wasn't a deep red color like I expected. It was a white one, but she said that it was ripe enough to eat. When I put it in my mouth thinking it would be bitter, it wasn't. There was a huge amount of sweetness that radiated from it. It was quite good.

"Very good," I said with my mouth half full of a few more.

"I like to pick these for pies."

"We like apple pies where I come from." My throat thickened with the shift to memories of home.

"Apple pies? We eat apples, but I've never made an apple pie."

I was about to give myself away and bring up the Blue Bell ice cream fetish I had that went with apple pies, but I caught myself. Instead, I just smiled. It felt like I was talking to a friend from back home. Truly, it was nice.

****

Morning after morning over the next slowly passing days in the gardens were the best time, though. I spent a few mornings just sitting and watching the dew dry from the leaves. Julia would show up mid-mornings after breakfast was done. She was always beaming with an electric smile. I started to look forward to her company every morning.

"Do you grow tomatoes here?" I asked one morning.

"Tomatoes? I've never heard of that. I got a case of peaches for the first time from Persia yesterday, and I don't know much about them."

"I'd love to help with that." Since I was familiar with them, I told her all about them. "The main thing is to let them sit for a little while after being picked and don't forget to remove the pit. I'll be more than pleased to handle the peaches. I will enjoy having more to do."

"Thank you," she said and beamed with something unspoken.

"What is it?" I asked.

"Are you with child?"

"What? No. No chance in Hell." I wouldn't explain my IUD or that I hadn't had relations with a man in several years. I just left it at no.

"Hell?"

"Hades, as you call it here."

"Hmm. Well I'm sorry to ask, but you are glowing like you are." We walked to get water for the daffodils that were wilting. Then she became solemn. "I was promised to a man once." And there it was. The sorrow that held her eyes captive.

"Really? What happened?"

"He just left one day. Told his family that he had to travel somewhere. Then, he was gone."

"I'm sorry." Julia's beauty showed more when she was sad. Her bottom lip protruded in an innocent way, and her eyelashes fluttered as if to control the pain.

"No, it is fine. He was a good man, though. I was beguiled by him. There was no one else for me after him, because I had already gone passed the marrying age."

"Oh, but you seem so young." I was in disbelief. She did seem young. Not so much in her looks, but more so because of her simple thoughts and ways.

"Yes, he left when I was twenty. After twenty, suitors don't come around anymore. And then my father died and left me with nothing. So without a dowry, your chances of marriage decline to almost nothing." She still looked sad but smiled anyway.

We talked some more, and then she got to work clipping and pruning for the day. She attended to some of the marigolds and roses closer to me. She had a nice touch and gentle way about her. After the sun would reach the second half of the sky, the cooks would come to carry out of the gardens, thyme and rosemary for the evening meal. When they clipped it, I could smell the fresh aroma of the leaves like they were already in a decadent sauce or stew. It always made me hungry. I actually loved my time in the gardens.

In the afternoons, I learned how to spin wool, which was a central domestic occupation for women of these times. Aida had a Jewish woman by the name of Livia teach me. She had grey hair braided down her back. And a stern personality, which I learned immediately. Remembering my first encounter with her, I disliked her. "Aida, why do you bring anyone up here? You know I like to work alone," she told an agitated Aida.

Aida pressed, "Well begin to enjoy company. This is my friend Kyla, and you will need to show her how to spin."

I sat down next to Livia excited with anticipation. She frowned at me. "So where are you from?" She had a mocking tone, but I ignored it.

"I'm from Hebron."

"No, you are not a Jew. I know my fellow Jews."

"Excuse me?" Who was she to know what I was?

"You look to be someone always searching. Jews don't search; we just know."

"Know what?"

"We know what God's path is for us, and we embrace it. You..." She stopped spinning to point at me. "You look like you wouldn't know it if He sent it with a starling and let the little bird excrete it on your head!"

I couldn't help myself. I laughed at the metaphor and she did too.

The next couple of visits, I grew to admire the old hag. And I took to spinning fairly easily. Suddenly, housewife-like duties appealed to me. But my entire upbringing was about avoiding them. Go to college, get a career, and pay someone else to do these things for me. Yea, it was all drilled into me.

One afternoon, Livia was working on something quite beautiful. I paused at the threshold to watch in wonder. Before I made my presence known, I saw a tear or two drop down her cheek. "Livia, are you alright?"

She dropped her hands and turned to me as though she was unaware of what I was talking about. "I'm fine my dear. Good day to you."

"I saw you crying."

She paused and her shoulders stayed curled forward. "Today, I have learned of some tragic news." Her voice was quiet and laced with dread.

"Tell me, maybe I can help."

"Oh no, I wouldn't burden you with my problems." She turned back to her work.

"I insist. Let me help you. You must."

She looked down at her sandaled feet, and her eyes softened. My husband, Gidan, may have to sell our land. The crops are not producing as much anymore and the neighboring farmer grows tired of loaning us supplies for our farm and animals. Gidan is insisting that the new crop he has planted will produce a bountiful harvest. But our neighbor, Eli, does not agree."

"Tell me why." My interest was piqued. This was what I was good at. I could finally be of some use. I listened as she told me of the new crop, rice of all things, and how they had learned how to prep the land from a Chinaman during trade. The act of puddling the soil puzzled Gidan but intrigued the gambling side of him immensely. Therefore, he bought the seeds and started on the next harvesting cycle. I smiled to myself as I recollected how my distant family in Texas were major rice farmers. I couldn't believe that what was discovered from China by Livia's husband was still in use in my time.

A day or two later I was convincing Livia and Gidan to allow me a meet with their neighbor, Eli. Gidan, with his long grey beard and wrinkly, sun damaged skin, was hesitant but felt he had nothing left to lose. Once he decided it was worth a try, he was out of sight preparing a way to secure us a meeting before I could talk with him more about his ideas. I decided to fall back on my own memories and knowledge of what I gained from my distant family back home and the rules of business I learned over the years. Devising a plan of action came quickly, and I began practicing my sales pitch for the rest of the day.

After the meeting was set, I prepared with Aida on what to wear. I knew that my singular advantage in the negotiations was to appear prominent and capable with Aida's influence and help. We selected a rich, dark green gown with gold fringes and tall neckline to accentuate my face. I needed to appear more loyal than an average commoner.

Viggo volunteered to travel with me by carriage to the fields outside of town. Which was a good thing. I needed another man to move the conversation along if needed.

The Gidan's land was bigger than I expected. As we made our way over the small hill, I could see for miles across his land. It was stunning to behold with its rich green pastures and small creeks. We continued on until we came to another stretch of land with sheep so sporadically spread out all over its pasture that I wasn't sure how we'd get through. With the sun beaming down brightly, I noticed the small home settled to the right of the path with plants growing up the walls giving it a deserted feel. But as we came closer, a big, older man came out and my breath hitched in my chest. I had to remind myself that I could do this. And I would for Livia.

After we did the greeting formalities, Eli wasted no time. "I will speak to you because you are Viggo's friend. However young lady, I will warn you that I am not pleased to be speaking to a woman in matters of business." Eli was straight to the point as we sat down at the rickety table. I didn't allow it to bother me. I was on a mission.

"Well, thank you for changing your mind. What I have to tell you would not only benefit Gidan but also you." I said while taking in the small room and the squeamish older lady pouring us tea that I assumed was his wife. The younger man that stood beside Eli with dark judgmental eyes appeared to be impatient with me though I did not yet know why. I studied him for a second and ascertained by his features that he was Eli's son. I made a point to keep that in mind throughout my visit with the desire to tread lightly in case the son held any say in the proceedings.

Viggo chimed in while I was scheming, "Either way Eli, I am very thankful for your kind hospitality."

Nodding at Viggo, Eli countered, "So how could this benefit me?"

I sparked an interest quicker than I thought. "The crop that Gidan has discovered from China is a robust crop. If he is successful, which I know he will be, it has the potential to feed several towns three times over each season. And I have a proposition that would benefit you as well." I hoped I said *proposition* correctly in their language. My breath caught while I waited to see.

"Really?" His greedy eyes gave him away. He liked what I said.

"Yes, I know a lot about rice from my travels. There is no denying it is a risk in this soil. But Gidan now has the knowledge of how to procure the soil to make this very doable."

"How?"

Gidan begins to inform his neighbor about the technique that will be used as I studied Eli's son. The young man had started to nervously tap the table but did not speak out of respect for his father. But what did it matter to him?

When Gidan was done and Eli seemed impressed, Eli turned to me. "So once again, how will this help me?"

"We just need you to continue your assistance to Gidan for one more harvest. If the crop takes and flourishes, then Gidan promises to cut you in on the profits plus reimburse you for your passed generosity." I noticed Gidan look down both out of a slight disgrace but also with a questioning look that told me I maybe should have consulted him on this proposal before the negotiating began.

"How much?" Eli leans forward.

"Ten percent of the profit." I'm winning! "And if it doesn't work, Gidan agrees to sell his land to you without question. I did hear right that you were the one asking to buy?"

"Yes."

"Good, then it's a win win for you either way."

"Twenty, and I will waive any repayment of services rendered."

I looked over to Gidan, and he nodded a subtle yes.

"You have a deal." I beamed. Both men and Viggo stood and shook hands as I took in what just transpired. I was successful in helping Livia! I couldn't be happier at that moment.

As the men talked some more and celebrated with wine and cheery dispositions, I asked to excuse myself to get some fresh air. Around the side of the house, I walked a short distance to admire the family barn. It was built bigger than the home and much sturdier. After my success, I was feeling a little more adventurous. So I wondered in through the slightly opened door.

Inside, it was dusty and hot with the setting sun barely lighting the space. It took a moment for my eyes to adjust. And then suddenly the hairs on the back of my neck stood up. I turned to find Eli's son glaring at me. Trying to keep it light, I smiled. "Well hello. It was a nice day for a walk, and I just thought a moment out of the sun would refresh my senses."

"You, Roman whore. What have you done?"

"Excuse me. I'll just be getting back." I tried to push by him, but he shoved me back into a table I didn't notice there before. Fear crept in, but I knew screaming would be futile. I was too far from the house.

His thick brows pinched together and his breathing sped up. "You heard me, Roman whore. You ruined everything. I was supposed to be given Gidan's land after my father purchased it. It was going to be me and my fiancé's home!"

"I'm sorry but right now my allegiance is to Gidan. I didn't realize that you had a stake in it." I paused hoping for some sympathy. But stirring in my mind were three things: the jerk called me a whore, I was suddenly classified as a Roman, and oh God he had just pulled out a knife. "Listen, we can talk this over."

"You've done enough talking, woman." He lunged toward me with the knife, and I jumped out of the way. I grabbed a large pot and threw it at him. He dodged it and sliced open my upper arm with the dull, rusty blade. I bent over in pain and tears formed in my eyes. He was going to kill. And there was no-one around to save me. My hero was off in another town, and there were no police to call.

As he stood before me, I realized my predicament and how if I continued to do what a 1st Century woman would do to protect herself, he'd be ready for it. I had to think outside the box. I had to do something that he would not be expecting. I looked around for another weapon while my mind went in circles. No, no, he would just over power me again.

He stepped forward. Then, I looked up and my eyes caught sight of the three by three-inch beam just above my head and the thought hit me. Immediately, I jumped up to grab the beam, swung out, and kicked him to push him back giving me enough time to execute the gymnastic parallel bars' move I learned when I was a kid. As he was recovering from my kick, I swung higher and pulled my hips up against the beam. Once in that position, it took me no time to lift my leg over it, jump up, and balance beam my way to the end of the barn. Thankfully, the two or so seconds that it took for him to comprehend what I had done, gave me the chance to bolt to the window. I forced the window open, jumped on the unsteady roof, and jumped to the ground into a roll I learned from gymnastics too. Moving my feet as fast as I could, I ran and ran until I made it back to the safety of my friends.

****

"You are cut deep. The important thing is to clean it before it festers." Livia was so efficient without having ever stepped foot in a medical school. Before I knew it, I was bandaged up and feeling like I may survive the day's events.

"Thank you, Livia."

"No, thank you. I will always be grateful for your help. I am just so sorry for what happened. Eli's son has been brought in for questioning by the village counsel. You will never have to worry about him again. Even Eli extends his apologies. Now, you must go get some rest when we're done. The traveling back here drained much of your blood. My husband knows nothing of how wounds should be treated. I am still aggravated that he wrapped your arm in an old blanket. He knows better than that. That's how he lost half his leg many moons ago."

"No worries. I'm just glad to be back home." I took in Aida's house again as Livia and Aida fussed over me. It did actually feel like home, and I smiled to myself at the comfort it brought me. On top of that, I saved my own hide without my soldier friends. Maybe I am not so much a damsel in distress. Either way my thoughts went to Eriksen. If anything, I wanted so badly to share with him my heroism.

I stood on weak legs while Livia braced me under my arm. I had lost a lot of blood. "Maybe I should sit back down."

Aida motioned for me back to the wooden bench. "Kyla, I will send for food."

Livia smiled. "That is probably for the best before she takes rest. I'll stay here with her."

It seemed like Aida jogged out of the room. My head was spinning, so everything played on my eyes funny.

Livia reached into a bowl and pulled out a damp cloth. "Here, my dear. Your face looks gaunt." She wiped gingerly with the rag across my clammy skin. It didn't help the attack that was brewing.

"I'm fine. I just get sick like this when I get stressed or injured." I didn't know if I said *stressed* or *injured* correctly in their language. I didn't care at that point. I was falling into another panic attack. The second one since we found ourselves in this time. I should count myself lucky, I had been through a lot and had only suffered two so far. And the fact that these two women said something about losing a lot of blood, didn't help. I think I freaked.

Aida came running back in with bread. I broke off a piece and tried to chew it, but my mouth was too dry. I couldn't swallow it. She then handed me some water and addressed Livia with a higher pitched voice. "Is it the wound?"

Livia wiped my face again. "No. Something else."

I bent over at the waist to lay over my knees and started my slow breathing techniques. I heard Livia speak to Aida again. "Do you have any lavender or sage close?"

Aida must have left again because there were no more sounds in the room. And all I felt were Livia's ministrations on my neck and arms. "There, there."

My heart rate was screaming through my chest. I couldn't hear or comprehend anything else around me. Then, I smelled the lavender, a sweet floral scent. It had been broken up and put in the small bowl of water. Livia was now wiping it all over my exposed skin. I couldn't believe how much something so simple was helping. My racing heart slowed down to a steady, comforting beat. The sweat that poured from my pores was wiped away. I sat up and saw relief cross my friends' faces.

With a shaky voice, I said, "I'm fine now. I may have to hold on to that lavender for now on if you don't mind, Aida."

"Not at all. I will put some in a pouch for you. Now, let's get you to the bed for some rest."

I didn't argue.

Chapter 9

The days continued on and there still was no word from the Senator or my friends. We had lunch served one day on the patio because the breeze off the Mediterranean was so relaxing. I thought to myself that I could have lived in Tripoli for the rest of my days. It was quite nice. However, I would start to miss my cousin and even my mom before I entertained the idea of staying any further. And the ever present danger reminded me that trying to get home should be my first priority.

"A woman can not function in a Roman society without a man overseeing her," Aida pointed out to me as we ate. "Your father doesn't have a suitor lined out for you?" She probed gently. Aida with her countenance so befitting for this Roman elegant life. I couldn't picture her anywhere else. She would never had survived a day with her captives.

"He didn't believe I needed to marry just yet." I lied. I just wasn't sure what to say.

Ignoring my father's false wishes, she continued. "There is a good Roman family here that has a second born son that may suit you. Would you allow me to invite them over for dinner one night? A good man could protect you and afford you the respect you need to keep attackers at bay."

Without an excuse on hand, I had to accept. "Yes, I guess it couldn't hurt."

Increasing sounds of movement flowed onto the patio. "Your grace, Senator Nicator has returned," said Panak, Aida's Egyptian slave.

I jumped up and ran through the villa straightening my hair as best I could. When I got to the door, no one was there. Panak came up behind me with a bow. "If you are looking for your friend, the one named Erikson, he said he was going to the gardens to look for you." I tried not to look too excited as I dashed back through the house and out onto the terrace.

I saw Julia at the herb garden notice me moving toward Eriksen, so she slipped back inside to give me privacy. He was turned with his back toward me. He had a restless stance. I did not want to act like it was a big deal to see him. So, I slowly walked around the budding trees as if to check their progress.

When he saw me, he nodded. I nodded back. "Oh, you're here."

"Yes," he said with a pensive expression.

"Why and where did you go?"

"To Macedonia with the Senator. He sold it to us by saying he felt that he needed to thank me and my men further for our help with his cousin. He wanted to treat us well and show us Rome's immense hospitality." I could hear the Senator saying those exact words. "I knew something was amiss, but we had to gather more intel before we reacted." He was kicking something at his feet. With his head tilted down, he moved his eyes back up at me.

"I'm glad you're back." Dangit, I didn't know why I said that.

"Me too."

"I've worried about you guys. I had trouble sleeping because of it." I revealed timidly and internally cursed myself for it.

"I haven't slept well either."

"I thought you would never come back. That I would be left here alone in this time without anyone who really knew me. You kind of were always there. I could count on it; you know?"

"You did?" His face perked up.

I smiled briefly. "Yes. So why are you glad to be back? If you're just following the mission. Why would you be glad to be back? And come out here looking for me? Little ole me, the problem child."

"We were pretty much done there. But...I guess I'll be blunt. I did decide to rush back. For several reasons. I won't tell you all of them but one." He sucked in his breath and proceeded slowly, "Do you know what you're doing to me?" His eyes glossed over.

"You're kidding me, right? That doesn't sound like you." I sat down on the bench playing coy.

He shook his head no and moved a little closer to me. "The last few weeks, I've thought, pretty much all about you. And of the night you walked into that dining room in that pale blue dress..." He pinched his nose and stood staring down at me.

"What? That was a long while ago. You're still thinking about that, not what I did?"

"No, I haven't had my mind these nights on what you did. Not that at all." He clenched his jaw and looked around. Then, he approached closer in such an empowering way that I had to avert my eyes. He sat down looking at me, but he was extremely close to me. I watched him swallow slowly again. His lips then came within inches of mine. I willed him to kiss me as I looked up at his gorgeous blue eyes. This big guy even licked his own lips giving me shivers. He leaned down and touched his lips to mine. I almost jumped back in disbelief. I couldn't believe what I was doing or him.

He took a breath and reached his hands into my hair releasing it down to my shoulders. When he saw my eyes close in a submissive way, he slowly eased farther into the kiss. His lips were so soft, and I moaned at their movement. He tilted his head to get a better angle and moved his tongue into my mouth with such a tender gesture that was so foreign and strange for this man.

I melted instantly and pushed my body into his chest. My delicate limbs seemed to disappear into his bulky build. I almost passed out from the passion it ignited in me. His smell, his taste, his sultry mouth, the safety I felt around him and was so glad to have back; all were driving me crazy. I went to reach up to his face, but he shifted back and grabbed my wrists shaking his head as if to shake me out of his system.

"What are we doing?" he said with a raspy voice. "What am I doing?"

"I ...I don't know." I bit my lip.

I noticed his face go soft again as he looked down at me and lowered his voice. "You don't know what you're doing to me."

"What?"

He shook his head again and got serious on me, "Just... Don't look at me like that." He smiled for a second and my heart dropped at his amazing good looks.

"Like what?" I said dumfounded.

His eyes were firm on me. "I kept telling myself to stop thinking about you. That this can't happen. Or maybe hoping you would slap me silly for trying."

I laughed. "I'm confused."

"I have to get my head back in the game, Kyla. Understand?" He tensed up again.

"Okay," I said with a sly grin. I couldn't help myself. I couldn't get over the fact that I had this kind of effect on him. No, wait, on a warrior. What was happening to me?

"Do you know what you're getting into Kyla?"

"What?" I asked and the sudden sensation of being flooded with warmth crossed my body.

"With me, with this mission, with all of it. You could have just stayed back, kept quiet, and lived like your princesses in your Disney movies, happily ever after." He fidgeted with his thumbs. "But then again, what am I doing?" he stood up and ran his hand through his hair. "Ugh, I can't think right now. I shouldn't have done that. It won't happen again."

"It's okay." I said innocently. And willed him to do it again and again. I had lost my mind.

He frowned at me. "Not just that but you don't know anything about me. If you were any other woman back in our time, I'd have tried to sleep with you by now."

I froze. Sudden heart palpitations caught my breath.

He continued, "I'm not innocent, Kyla. I don't think I'm who you think I am. None of us special ops guys are, hence the fact that I have a son I never see. I have a chaotic past. I wasn't all that responsible. You wouldn't like it. I just don't think I'm worthy... of someone like you yet."

I didn't know what to say.

"I want to be. I'm trying to take things slow and do things right for a change. But how can I? In the middle of all of this?" And he gestured to area all around us. "If we were anywhere but here. You are the woman I was wanting to better myself for. It's still just not the right time."

Then, he rested his right hand behind his neck. "And now things are getting real crazy. I still don't know if what you said the other night prompted the meeting in Macedonia with the Senator and one of Rome's commanders."

"What do you mean? I hardly said a thing or at least not anything important." I could feel an argument brewing on the cusps of the most awesome kiss I had ever had.

"You went into business mode that night and started telling the Senator how he could ease the tension between the Germans and the Romans. Women didn't talk politics back in the 1st Century. You could have made it obvious who you were to his consultant. And what happened to your arm?" He reached over his hand in a tender, protective way.

I shrugged him off not wanting to get into all that anymore. My mind was on his accusations. "Nothing. I'm fine. Politics? All I did was point out..." and then I paused trying to remember what exactly I did in fact say.

Eriksen squatted down right in front of me. Then, he lightly touched my knee and I caught him look at my lips. I instantly thought of our mistaken kiss. He looked back at my eyes. "You don't know what transpired at that table, do you?" When he said it in that way, I could see him back in our time with a baseball hat and fatigues on again.

"No."

"Were you that drunk?" he asked sharply.

His matter of fact, domineering tone lit me up. "Excuse me?"

"That was our missing scientist sitting next to you. Cyrus is our mission. Cyrus is Parker, our rogue scientist."

Instantly all that transpired back on Eli's farm. As well as the many nights I sat up at night trying to sleep out of worry for Eriksen ended up disappearing. "What? Why didn't you tell me that night?"

"Sshh." He put one long finger to my lips. I watched him lick his own lips again as if being this close to me was a real struggle for him. I melted. My insides turned to jelly as I hoped he'd kiss me again. Mad or not, I could get over it if I had his soft lips and huge hands wrapped all over me. Even though, he told me I was in the lair of the devil just a moment ago, my mind was not in the game either. And for the life of me, I still didn't know why it was focused more on the guy kneeling before me that I viewed as a simple grunt just a few weeks ago. "I didn't tell you because there are things you don't need to know," he added.

"What?" I whispered passed his finger.

"He didn't recognize us. But from his low talks with the Senator, he was making plans that night. I still don't know what yet. That is why we accepted the Senator's invitation to Macedonia. It turns out we got to see Parker and the Senator meet with one of Governor Varus' legionnaires. I had to determine what Parker's plans were and where he is keeping the vials before we take him out."

I stood up puzzled.

He continued, "You know the saying by Sun Tzu, 'Keep your friends close but your enemies closer'? We knew we had to go. And for the most part, we got some good intel. I was just worried that your slip up would bring awareness to Parker of who we were." He shrugged. "Although, we were told that Parker had friends on the inside that assured him he'd be the only one to be able to go through the machine."

My stomach lurched at that thought, and I turned to sit again. I was speaking to a potential mass murderer that day. I knew there was something familiar about him. He acted similar to us. We are from the same time, that was why. "So what else did your reconnaissance reveal? Do you know where the vials are?"

"We couldn't gage that, but we did discover that Cyrus offered the Senator something of high value or the Senator would not have continued to take him under his wing. And the meetings in Macedonia seemed to seal the Senator's protection over Parker." He took in the room again out of caution. "Kyla, I was in shock when he came into the dining room right before you with the Senator that night. What are the odds that we come across the cousin of a Senator that is in cahoots with our mission? I couldn't believe my eyes."

And then he turned back on the squadron leader, bossy routine. "Whatever happens now, you have to fly under the radar. With these people, with me. I'm not going to come see you again, okay?"

"I can't believe what I'm hearing." Not just hearing but what he was doing. He pretty much said he liked me but didn't want anything to do with me. "Now you're telling me you knew what was going on and you didn't tell me then. I can't get over that I was talking with a mentally ill man and you didn't even warn me. You left for weeks and told me *nothing*!"

He smiled down at me as he took a seat again. He put his arm around me. "Are you alright?"

"Yeah, I guess. Just taking it all in." I shrugged him off.

"What do you think me and my men were doing the whole time at dinner?

You were enjoying yourself while we were absorbing and planning."

"Oh, I feel like a moron." Not just about not knowing who Cyrus was. But for falling for the sexy moves he had just been playing on me.

"You didn't know. Remember we were briefed on Parker. You were not. You just accidently stumbled in on this whole thing. But it was your quick thinking with Viggo that got us this close. I don't know if we would have gotten this close to Parker if we didn't help Viggo."

"It's just a coincidence."

"I don't know Kyla. Pretty big coincidence. Did you know that the Israel army was planning to come in on West Bank Labs the next day to shut them down? The company was going to have to shut it all down."

"No, that's not true. I had until Sunday to fix it. And I had some good PR ideas. I was sure of myself."

He shook his head. "No, we were called in to do this mission sooner than planned because of the movement in their government. At this point in our time, the labs are already closed. We are the last hope to stop this maniac. Why do you think the men and I felt no choice but to kill you when you showed up in the cave? You were too risky. The mission too important. Either way, I'm sorry for hitting you on the head."

"Wait, wait... labs closed? That means the machine is shut down. Does that mean that there is no return home?" I didn't even pay attention to that last reminder he brought up about what happened in the cave.

"Yes, my men and I knew that this was a one-way trip. I'm sorry that you didn't."

"No, no, no. This can't be true." My head started spinning, and I pulled away from him sweating immensely. He caressed my shoulders and pulled my hair back in a tender way that I almost forgot that I was trapped in another time. But I didn't. The anxiety started to climb through my body. I pushed him away and rushed out of the garden with tears streaming down my cheeks. I barely waved hi at Aida as she came around the corner saying she was coming to check on me.

When I got to my room, I closed my door and collapsed on my bed in tears. I cried and cried until I heard a knock at my door. I didn't want to answer it. I didn't want to see or have anything to do with him. I wanted to go to sleep and wake up back at home. The knock came again, and I touched my lips. That jerk actually kissed me. Kissed me and then said he regretted it. Yea, well I didn't need another commitment phobic man in my life. It was for the best. For the best for what? What was I going to do since I had just learned that I was stuck in the first century?

With unsteady hands, I pushed myself off the bed. I moved toward the door with the thoughts of a tall, blonde soldier waiting on the other side for me to yell at some more.

****

It was not what I wanted on the other side of the door. I gasped as two large men in Roman uniforms grabbed me and pulled me down the hall. When I began to scream, they slapped me and yanked me harder. Through the commons area and then the foyer, I kicked and screamed. Then, we were out the front door.

An even taller soldier was standing outside waiting. "Kyla Marshall, my name is Decurion Jacobus. You have been turned over into our care for your trip to Venice."

"Venice, what are you talking about?" I screamed, "Eriksen!"

The soldier to my left slapped me again. "Be careful with her Iulius. She can't be damaged."

"I demand to know what is going on, a-hole!"

"A pole? Young lady that is definitely not my name. I said Jacobus."

And then I spit in his face.

"Control yourself woman, there is much at stake for you and your friend." He looked behind me. "Ah Senator, maybe you can enlighten her."

The Senator was coming up with an angry Aida at his heels arguing with him. "Cousin, I agreed to come along with the promise that you would not harm her."

"Aida, finish packing your things and meet us on the cart," he told her and then turned to me. "You see young lady, we are Romans and you are not. You are a Jew. You demand nothing from us."

I halted in my struggling. "We saved her when no Romans were to be found."

"Yes, I know and for that I am thankful. That is why I'm giving you a choice now."

"A choice?" I hissed.

"Yes, either stay here and spend your days with my family or come to Rome and help your new home become greater. You see, we want to give you full citizenship if you will do what your empire asks of you."

"And what is that?"

"Enter into a matrimonial union with our bordering countrymen, the Germanic people. See it was your great mind that gave me the idea."

"Never!!"

He went on without flinching. "It is a shame though because you would have made an enticing bride for a nobleman in Rome with your unmatched beauty, but I would not have received as much favor from that union as I will with this."

"Are you deaf a-hole? I said no!"

"She makes no sense," said Jacobus by his side.

The Senator looked at him and back at me again. "Ah, well maybe if I clarify, it will help. Your choice is to marry the tribe leader's son that we have negotiated with and in return your friend, Eriksen, will live. Embarrass Rome with your refusal, and we kill him now." He nodded to Jacobus.

"Legionnaire Nero, please bring forward the man. Thank you," Jacobus said.

Suddenly four more legionnaires appeared pulling a chained up man with them. It was Eriksen! It looked like he did not come easily. He was beaten up pretty badly but inwardly I smiled, because so were the four legionnaires pulling him our way. When they got closer, they pushed him to his knees and he looked up and smiled a half grin. I imagined he was a tough one to dominate. Then the shorter soldier on his right pulled a small dagger out and put it to Eriksen's neck.

Senator Nicator spoke again, "Now, what is your decision?"

I looked back and forth between Eriksen and the Senator.

"Come on, we have a ship waiting for us at the port that we must catch. What is your decision?"

Eriksen spoke, "Kyla, don't worry about me." And then he spit blood to the side. "Stay with Aida here where you are safe, like I told you. Screw them and their scheming."

I frowned and dropped my eyes to the ground. I couldn't lose him. I was mad at him, but I couldn't lose him. 'Live to fight another day' was all my mind was saying. I had to help him live. Then, as the dagger pierced into his skin, I said, "Wait! I will marry into that tribe as long as you promise me one thing."

"What?" asked the Senator.

"Promise me that I can talk to him whenever I want to." And I pointed at the man kneeling on the ground that was giving the soldier with the dagger a deathly glare.

The Senator smiled then and waved his hand toward the legionnaire threatening Eriksen. "How about once on the ship to Venice and then another time if he survives the games?"

"Games, what games?"

"Well in order for him to live, I must still do something with him. After all, he is a danger to my plans. I will let him live, but he will be sold to a lanista in Venice and be well cared for."

"What is that?" I said trying not to shed the tears swimming in my eyes.

"He will be a gladiator. And judging by his fighting ability already, I imagine he will be a great one. The ladies will be infatuated with this one. I know I will get a good price for him."

"No!" was all I managed to say as they dragged me to the first cart behind the two lead horsemen. In my anger toward Eriksen, I never thought we'd be separated like this. And deep down I hated the mission and wished he would have too. Maybe he would have looked at me differently. But would I have respected or cared for him the same way if he did forsake it and stopped following the scientist.

I looked back and saw the Roman soldiers tie Eriksen to the back of a second cart with plans to make him follow on foot. My breathing sped up and I had to look away to calm myself. Just then, Aida and Viggo joined me on the cart and I wasted no time, "Where are my other men?"

They both looked at each other frowning and back at me. Viggo spoke first, "Kyla, they never returned with Eriksen. He told us they had to return home to Hebron." With that, I feared the worse. They quit the mission. They abandoned us.

Chapter 10

That night we were at the Port of Tripoli and loading onto a galley style boat with easily over a hundred paddles sticking out of the sides and two giant sails. It had a narrow hull and was completely made of wood. I boarded paying close attention to where they were taking Eriksen; down to a lower deck.

From the chatter around me, I figured out that the boat was a Phoenician merchant ship. Decurion Jacobus made several trades with the Phoenicians in order to catch a ride on this trade ship that was headed to Egypt and then on to Venice. The ship was loaded with close to ten tons of copper and fifty marines manning the paddles. The Phoenicians were skilled in traveling across the tumultuous Mediterranean and had been doing it for close to a thousand years. And could do it in record time. The total trip was expected to take over eight to ten days depending on weather conditions.

"Lady, you must retire for the night. We have many days of traveling ahead." The man before me had curly black hair and a dark complexion. I didn't expect anyone to speak to me as I watched the land grow smaller and smaller when we pulled away from the dock.

"I feel better being where I can see. Are you Roman?"

He stared down his nose at me. "Mostly. I prefer to be known as a Canaani. I am the Captain of this ship."

"Glad to meet you, my name is Kyla."

"Kyla, I am Si." He smiled then turned away. "Now please leave the deck with your friends. We are not comfortable with having guests, especially women. Women are bad luck on a ship." He seemed innocent enough but demanding. And his own funny sounding Latin was hard to follow. The accent being flat, no inflection.

"I'm sorry Si, but I have never ridden on something like this before and it scares me. I'll stay right here."

Si turned back toward me. "Fine. But it is the best ship. The Romans still can't replicate something this great." He walked off and I put it together that Canaani was actually what we called Phoenicians. That would explain him being uncomfortable with visitors on his boat, especially Roman soldiers. These Phoenician sailors lived on boats and traveled from port to port never actually speaking to outsiders. I witnessed it when we arrived at Egypt two moons later.

The boat anchored at high noon close the Egyptian shore. I went on deck to watch several sailors abort the boat and get into a smaller boat with crates of mixed pottery. Though it was quite far onto shore, I could make out them leaving their goods on the ground and proceeding back to their smaller boat to wait.

"Si, you're just going to leave your things there? What about payment?" Being a business person by nature, I just had to ask.

He looked at me with questioning brows. He was trying to decide if I was worth his breath. "When they come, if they like, they take and leave gold in place of the crates. If they don't like, they just leave our items there."

"Oh, well what if they like, take, and don't leave money." I asked the obvious question.

He turned and looked down at me perplexed now. "Well, that could possibly happen. We just won't leave till we get paid then. No one wants to do such a thing because it is not honorable and makes for bad trade relations. And we have good things that these people want."

Trade relations? Supply and demand? All the foundations to our modern business dealings. However, these people never had to speak with each other to gain a benefit. They let the product sell itself. No cost of advertising, negotiating, analyzing of data, nothing. Just a simplistic and uncomplicated early form of business. It was rather interesting.

"See, here they come." A small group of Egyptians, darker skinned than the Phoenicians, came across the hill carrying something in bags.

I asked, "It's good, isn't it? They must know you do good business because they are carrying something to leave you."

"Yes, yes. But we always do. See this is our livelihood. How we support our families and for some of us, our bad habits." He grinned at one of his smaller sailors who stumbled onto the deck and ambled toward us. "Kyla, this is Tate my right hand man... sometimes."

Tate was a shorter man and probably in his fifties. He grinned from ear to ear with not but a handful of teeth. "Ah Kyla. I've had dealings with the Persians. You are a violent sort."

"No, Tate. The woman is a Jew."

"Ah, I've had dealings with the Jews. I still remember the night I had with one. Oh, she was beautiful. And that's all I remember until the next morning when I woke up to a hay stack that smelled just like her."

Si rolled his eyes which surprised me because I thought that was more of a modern expression. "You would be best not to tell Kyla anymore of your fantasies or fake exploits."

"Hmm." And he walked off scratching his head with his pants barely hanging on below his protruding belly. I kind of liked him.

"Tate's had a rough life."

"What happened?" I stepped aside as his men came back on board with the Egyptian bags.

He looked at me surprised. "We're a dying race, Kyla."

"What do you mean?"

"Our home is still in Carthage and we're able to dock there, but it is not ours anymore. Why do you concern yourself with this?"

I ignored his question. "Africa, right? Carthage, Africa?"

"Yes."

"Who does it belong to?"

"Rome! It has been like that for over one hundred years. My ancestors passed down stories of how great our empire was once before the Romans. Now, we are here and there barely being granted passage to secure our livelihood."

He continued while looking out onto the coastline. "Tate hates Romans. He's been in many brawls with them."

"Brawls from what?"

"Gambling. He can be difficult sometimes. And he likes to play too much. But he is the best man I ever met." I smiled inwardly at the camaraderie between these two unlikely men.

"So you have a family, Si?"

"Yes, a wife but no baby. The gods have willed it not so." There was a banging noise and I heard Tate yell to the other men, "No, I bet one ounce of my finest that the bird won't bite after my sweet talk." There was a 'yes' and many 'nays', and the next thing I heard was, "Ahhh... she bit me!" And the sailors cheered at his expense. Trying not to laugh, I looked back at Si, who kept his eyes forward not paying attention to the usual raucous on his ship.

"I'm sorry."

"Sorry? Sorry for what? You are not one of the gods." He looked dumbfounded at my choice of words.

"Oh, I just meant... Nothing, never mind." I wasn't sure how to word it. "Do you trade all year?"

"No, we can not. The sea gets too unstable. We can only sail between spring and fall. So we just have two seasons to make our bounty." I nodded my understanding.

A boy not older than my nephew ran by me with a mop. Si hollered to him, "Malum! Come here."

When the boy walked up close, I noticed the burn marks covering one side of his young face. He addressed his Captain, "Yes, sir?"

"Malum, fetch me and my friend some potable water."

Malum looked at me with deep set, dark eyes before he jetted back off.

I turned back to Si. "A young boy on these voyages too?"

Si nodded. "He was found on one of our trade ones awhile back. He had been left by the Turkish shore and badly hurt. I took him in and healed his wounds."

"How old is he? Does he not have family?"

"The Romans destroyed his village and killed his family. He got away. But he was one of the few that did. He is thirteen."

Why was I suddenly emotional over that boys' situation? "I thought he was younger. But that is sad."

"He's been with us for a few years. He is now at the age that he can do almost everything my men do. This will be good labor for him."

Malum returned with a small wooden cup of water. I sipped enjoying the hydration. Malum watched every move I made.

Si put his cup down on a barrel beside us. "Malum, this is our guest. Her name is Kyla."

Malum stood almost about my height and his confident face and thin beard gave away his older age more so now that he stood so close. He kept his head down and looked at me once. "Nice to meet you. Are you with the Romans?" A hint of venom escaped from his voice.

"Yes, but I am not willingly."

"Oh."

Si noticed his men boarding back on the boat and gave to order to head out before turning back to us. "Malum, she will be with us for a few days."

The boy asked, "A woman?"

I frowned. "Why? Is that a problem?"

He replied, "No. Just..."

Si interrupted, "He doesn't really see many women. Or hasn't in a few years. He stays on the ship at ports."

Malum rubbed his hands on his pants. "You're beautiful."

I laughed. "Thank you. I am glad you think so."

Si looked to the west and turned back toward me. "You need to go below, there is a storm brewing."

Then, he addressed the young boy. "Malum, see to it that she has what she needs down below to ride out the storm. Make it quick. I need you back up here."

Above and all around me were the tell tale signs of impending rain. The clouds were rolling in darkening the previous baby blue sky and the waves were getting restless. I pulled my hood over my head and followed Malum to the lower deck where I found Aida sitting cross legged with Leta fanning away the heat for her. I couldn't bring myself to talk to Aida still, so I walked passed her and found an alcove where I could ride out the storm.

Malum kneeled beside me. "Mistress Kyla, if there is anything else you need you only have to ask."

Boy was he a flirt. "Thank you, Malum. I am fine."

A boyish smile appeared on the untouched side of his boyish face before he retreated back to the ship's deck.

I felt the boat rock on the sea as the waves got more violent. Leta began to cry from worry. I spoke before standing, "It will be okay; these boats can handle worse." I went to sit next to Leta so I could talk to her more. I heard Tate singing on the top deck like the storm wasn't a big deal. "It's not even a big storm." *Boom.* The sound came from the starboard side and the boat shook and creaked. She huddled into me while Aida grabbed Viggo by the arm. A small leak developed above our heads and a trickling of rain water dropped into our quarters. "I've never liked the seas. Never!!" Leta cried and her eyes danced all around.

I thought of Eriksen tied up somewhere below us and wondered if he was worried or if sea life was second nature to him being that he grew up so close to it. I wondered if his family fished sometimes since he wore a fishing logo hat the first time I met him. I never asked him much about his childhood. He knew more about me than I did about him. I wish we had more time. If only I had gotten a chance to know him back at home, in our time.

I started to worry as Leta cried in my arms and Tate's out of tune singing stopped. I knew I lost Eriksen, and I hated our luck for it. No matter how hard we tried, negotiated, and remained patient. No matter how much of our blood, sweat, and tears we gave, we would not get any chance at a relationship or success at our mission. It was all out of our control. We were in an unpredictable and unstable existence.

As the boat pitched from side to side, I felt more helpless than I had ever felt in my whole life. I let the abusive rocking and thunder pound at my head and soul. The fear all around me was so palpable, it drew me in and strangled my resolve. I feared death but more so, I dreaded loneliness. Loneliness that would come in death and loneliness that would haunt me in life. A missing piece to my being that would and had always left me in despair. After what seemed like forever, the foundation of our earthly salvation finally settled into a steady and reliable motion. I released Leta to move to my small bed, and I cried myself to sleep.

****

"Come, my lady. Sit with me." Tate's early morning good mood after a night of hell was enticing. He pointed to a second wooden chair. There was a small table between it and his chair.

"Sure, is that coffee?"

"Coffee?" He questioned. Darn, shouldn't have gotten my hopes up. I survived the first week of withdraws to get to this point, but I'd gladly take addiction again for just one cup.

"Wine. Asian wine, the strongest. Want some?"

"How can you drink this early in the morning?"

He ignored me. "Watch woman Jew." He picked up the darkest pebble, threw it in the air, and shot his hand out to grab several pebbles that were left behind before catching his primary pebble. "See. Now you do."

It reminded me of Jacks. I picked up the same dark pebble and followed the same steps. When my hand shot out, I ended up knocking all the pebbles onto the wooden deck. "I suck!"

"I suck?" He looked bewildered at my English expression. I frowned and corrected myself in Latin, "I'm not good at this."

"Oh yes, yes you bad."

"Well, thanks."

"You have to toss the first pebble right over the existing ones so all your movement is in one spot. Much like life. Now try again." Was that advice from a drunk man?

I did as he said and did better. "Yes! I at least kept them on the table."

"The game is to not have them on the table but in your hand."

I laughed. It felt good to laugh.

"Can I ask you a question?" He said and his dirty tunic showed a trail of sweat down his middle.

"Sure." I looked up still laughing. "Go ahead."

"Why are you being escorted by Roman soldiers and a Senator?" He took a sip of his drink. He was sun tanned to the nines under that garment. Almost too much. He had a little build and fluffy, fuzzy eyebrows framing bird-like eyes.

"I'm to be married to a Germanic prince."

Tate spit his wine to the side. "Germans are savage."

"You said that about the Persians."

"Them too."

I giggled again.

He sobered for a second. "My wife died years ago. Best thing that ever happened to me."

"That's morbid."

The old widow shrugged his shoulders, nonplussed. "She wanted me to be a farmer and give this up." He pointed around at the ocean.

"I can see why you like it." The waves were almost silent. It was pretty relaxing. Two Roman soldiers came up on the deck and ruined my bliss. Tate noticed.

"Let's play another round," he said. I envied his life on his boat. His freedom. Something I took for granted back home in my time and in my country. The comical enigma went on to tell me about all his fun at bacchanals now that he was under the influence and in a sharing mood. "In vino veritas," I thought to myself as I listened to his stories.

****

After the game, I ate lunch with Malum. He brought me a plate of cured meat and sea biscuits. The meat was a little salty, but the biscuits were good. Malum sat cross legged with me on the wooden deck and kept his eyes on me as he ate. "Kyla, what do the Romans want with you?"

I swallowed the dry bread and placed my hands in my lap. "I am to marry a man from Germania."

"Do you not want to do that?"

"Women don't have choices in these times, Malum. I'm growing to accept that." I took a bite of the meat and yanked it with my teeth to tear it. "What did your parents do in Turkey?"

"Farmers."

"Did you have brothers and sisters?"

He wiped his upper lip with his arm. The boy was growing into his look. He was handsome when you looked passed his scars. "No. It was just me. Tate tells me that you have a friend in the holding cell down below."

I nodded. "A very close friend. He means the world to me."

"Do you not get to go see him?"

"Not yet. The Romans forbid me until they are ready for me to. I don't even know where he is being kept down there."

Malum's brow lifted. "But I do."

"Have you been down there?"

"I bring them their daily rations sometimes."

I scooted closer. "Did you see a really tall man with bright blue eyes?"

"I can't see their eyes. But there are not many down there."

"How are they doing?"

"Some are pretty bad off."

"Can you take me down there?" I asked hoping not to sound desperate.

He looked around. "I can in a few hours when the sun drops into the ocean."

"Thank you. That would be really nice of you. But, Malum."

"Yes?"

"The sun does not drop into the ocean."

He looked at me quizzically. "It looks like it does."

"Has anyone taught you how things work?"

"Work?" he asked.

My need to educate others, especially kids, almost got me in trouble. "Oh, I mean. How the sun works?"

"No, not really."

"We move around the sun. The sun is not here with us. It is far, far away."

"What do you mean when you say, we move around the sun?"

I demonstrated with my hands. One fist was the sun and the other fist was us. I moved us around the fist that symbolized the sun. "Like that."

"Oh."

I leaned in toward him. "Now, you have to promise me something."

"Yes, anything."

"Everything I tell you about these things must not be told to others."

"Why not?"

"They won't believe you."

"Is it all true?"

I smiled. "Oh, yes, Malum. It is definitely true." I took a breath and studied his scars. "How did you get the burns, Malum?"

He lifted his hand to cover his face and turned away.

I touched his hand. "Malum, I don't mean for you to hide them from me. They are not bad. I like you with or without them."

His dark eyes lit up when he looked back at me. "Really?"

"I think you are very handsome."

"I can't see how."

I pulled his hand all the way down and held it. "I do. And you are a very kind, young man."

"Thank you." He took a bite of the meat. "I got them when one of the legions attacked our farm. I was trying to protect my mother and was pushed away into the fire." He looked at our hands that were still touching. "I rolled out and managed to get free of it. They considered me dead and left me. My family traded with the Phoenicians. When my family didn't make it down to the shore for the annual trade, the Phoenicians thought we had nothing to trade. But they saw me on the shore dying and took me in."

"I am so sorry, Malum."

"Where do you come from?"

I removed my hand from him. "I come from a place way across the ocean. A place where we hardly ever worry about wars close to home. No one messes with us. Most battles are fought extremely far away."

"You must have a powerful army like Rome."

I smiled. "Oh, yes. We have the *best*, Malum. It is far better than Rome's. I wish I could show you one day."

"What is your home called?"

I licked my lips and wondered what it could hurt to tell him this. Then, I smiled again. "America."

Chapter 11

Malum had duties that night that kept him away. I couldn't go see Eriksen as I had hoped. I went to sleep upset. The storm that we sailed into around midnight didn't help either. I didn't know how many more storms at sea I could take.

The next day, nice singing made its way to us on the top deck. Malum took me down to the middle section of the boat but said it was the furthest we could go during the day. The middle space had two rows lined from stem to stern with men rowing in perfect unison. After the ferocious storm, the wind had died so much that the sails were ineffective in moving us along. Therefore, this led to the marines working harder than usual today. They were singing something that reminded me of a nursery rhyme but in their native tongue and with a higher tempo. When I first stepped down and they realized a woman was present, they quieted down but continued to sing and row with all eyes on me. They were darker skinned than I noticed upon boarding a few nights ago, and they didn't look like they were too mistreated. I took it all in wondering if I should have Malum take me back up the stairs when Legionnaire Nero, and another legionnaire I did not recognize, came down to fetch me. "Kyla, the Senator said you may have your chance to speak with your friend. I brought some water as part of his daily ration if you would like to give it to him."

Then, Nero spoke to Malum, "We will handle the prisoners today. Go back above deck."

"Yes, sir," Malum told them and looked wearily at me before leaving.

I followed Nero down another flight of steps to the lowest deck where most of the goods and other supplies were stored. As we came down, I immediately smelled the dingy, stagnant air. The legionnaires led me through a narrow aisle to the back of the boat and another smell hit my nose before I could make out what it was. It reminded me of the smell of septic tanks flushing out their sewer on the yards of homes back in Mississippi. Homes that were not on city lots and not connected with the city sewer plants. I always cringed when I visited those homes because the smell was overpowering in the summertime. I almost stopped dead in my tracks when the realization hit me of what that smell was.

However, for my desire to see Eriksen, I proceeded slowly on with the guard and saw men locked in cages staring angrily at me. Their faces were filled with dirt and their hair matted up. They all wore tattered pants but no shirts. It revealed the horror of old and new wounds across their chests and backs. I did my best not to show how uncomfortable I was at the sight of them.

As we moved farther down passed more cages, Nero motioned me to the right and into a cage smaller than my apartment closet back home. My eyes were still trying to adjust, but I could make out the body of man laid over on the floor. He started to sit up when the men pushed me in, locked the door, and moved back down the aisle to silence the other prisoners that started to yell at their Roman captors.

As the candle light aided my sight more, I saw that it was Eriksen. He looked similar to the other caged men, but his expressions and ice blue eyes set him apart. He had more blood over his body showing that his wounds were more recent and deeper. I didn't know what to say to him. My bottom lip trembled.

He took my hand and pulled me down to sit in front of him and he actually smiled, "Hello, it's good to see you."

Hello? I thought. How could he be so courteous right now? "What have they done to you?"

"Cheer up. I was tortured by Taliban much worse than this. Believe me."

Somehow, I didn't believe him. "Cheer up? What's going on Eriksen? Where did everything go wrong?" I asked him and noticed his lip was swollen and his face cut up as well. I wanted to kiss him softly on those lips in a way that could heal his pain or slap him and make it worse. But it seemed just having me there was enough for him. He didn't look like the same man that pushed me away the other day. I softened up to him, and I could tell it made him feel better.

"Lots. But it will all be alright."

"Stop making light of this. What happened?" I asked angrily.

"I'm to fight in the gladiator games, that's what."

I bit my lip. "I'm not just talking about that. But now that you bring it up, you do know how crazy that is. Those men fight for their lives and are trained just for that."

"And I am not? Remember you chose this; you must have some faith in me? I thought for sure you'd have them kill me on the spot. You were pretty mad at me that night. But to be honest, I was relying on it. I didn't want you to see me like this or put yourself in the situation you're in now. What were you thinking?" I listened to him talk and thought of the rough night I had just endured wanting so badly to have had him there holding me through it. Something I never wanted from a man before.

"I don't know." I wasn't about to tell him the truth. "But you're not afraid?"

"Of what? You marrying some other man?" Then he cringed in pain from a wound on his side.

"No, jerk. Afraid of fighting in the games? They fight with swords; you with guns."

"So you think special ops forces only get trained on guns? Kyla, what would happen if I was ambushed while I was positioned to neutralize a target? Do you think they trained us to turn and knock them in the head with my rifle?"

"I don't know." I knew he had some good fighting moves too. I had seen them when Aida was rescued, and when I was rescued. My stomach turned when the horror from that night overshadowed his heroic skills.

"Don't act so thrilled. Anyway, we're trained and conditioned for way more than that. And our country's special forces units primarily take the best." He paused to press into his side. "I was selected not only because of my military experience, but I was also on a Mixed Martial Arts team back home. I've won several awards." He winked at me.

My jaw dropped. "Gladiators wield a sword Eriksen. That's what 'gladiator' means. A man trained to fight with a sword. And that's way different!"

"I have pretty strong wrists and hands." He opened and closed his hands in front of me. "I got this." Then, he grinned from ear to ear at me.

"Whatever."

Eriksen's eyes turned cold and his tone deepened. "Special op soldiers are trained killers too, Kyla. Don't count me out yet." He looked so confident. A chill ran down my spine as I remember the hate in his eyes when he almost killed my attacker. He *was* a trained killer.

"You, military guys, are all the same- adrenaline junkie fools!" I stood to take a breath before I told him more of what I thought.

"I'm Christopher."

"What?" I turned back toward him shocked.

"My first name is Christopher. Christopher Gregory Eriksen."

"Okay..."

"I don't want to spend these last moments with you and you not know my whole name. Stop viewing me as just a military guy." He said with a somber expression that perked up my heart.

I kneeled back down by him enraged. "Ughh, stop talking like that. These can't be our last moments. You're scaring me. Tell me what's going on. There has to be something I can do."

"There is actually. But I don't know where to start."

"Just tell me it all. Stop keeping me in the dark."

He eyed me steadily and shifted in his spot to recollect all the events. "Well, I figured out some of what was going on before it happened. But it seems the Senator, in hopes of furthering his career, had connections with the former Governor of Syria, Varus. Publius Quinetilius Varus to be exact. And he wanted to strengthen that connection with these dealings that got us here and in this predicament. Dealings that started in Macedonia when me and my team traveled there without you. Now from what I understand, you are being delivered to Varus' men in Venice as a bargaining chip between the Romans and one of the Germanic tribes. Do you know what battle takes place in the region around the Lippe and Ems Rivers, around this time?" His mouth was dry, so it was difficult for him to finish his words. "Basically the Germanic territory? And do you know who Varus is?"

I forgot till then that Nero let me bring him some water, and I desperately handed it to him. He took it from me and gulped it spilling a few drops on to his bare chest. "No, I don't remember," I said.

He lowered the drained cup. "The Battle of Teutoburg Forest between the Germanic tribes and Rome. Rome lost. Rome was ambushed. I studied every war that was ever documented during my time in military school."

"So he wants to change the outcome? But why change one battle? This battle can't be any different than the slaughter of the Native American Indians in Trinity County, California in the 1800's or the battle of San Jacinto in Texas where they beat back Santa Anna and gained freedom from Mexico. If the Texans didn't win or weren't influenced to win because of the fall of the Alamo, then Mexico would own a few more hundred acres of land. What does all this matter? Who deserves the land anyway? And why change anything in human history? Everything has worked out to the better. We are now, for the most part, united under NATO because of WW2. And look at your team, men of different countries working together for the common good of the world under the UN. You said it yourself, each of your team's units served with each other in Afghanistan to fight the same battle."

I paused to lower my voice but continued on, surprisingly proud. "Men and women from countries all over our world are now fighting together against a faceless enemy or belief which is radical Islam. How amazing is that? Why would he want to change anything? I don't understand. I know I'm rambling. I'm just really stressed. And you know what, why not just warn Rome of the ambush? You said Rome lost because they were ambushed."

"You sure do babble much." His eyes smiled. "But that's just it. He doesn't want things to be the way they are in the 21st Century. And Varus wouldn't believe the Senator if he told him about the ambush made by Arminius anyway. In fact, Varus didn't believe Arminius' own father-in-law when he tried to warn Varus right before it happened or will happen. I guarantee that Parker knows all this. He's up to something else."

I became adamant. "Again why change this battle though?"

"Think about it. He brought up the theory of the domino effect that night in Tripoli. The effect as it stands now is good for our world because it resulted in a world connected. Connected in what way, Kyla?"

"Bettering of our world."

"But what makes us all see how the world needs to be? Who determines that?"

"Democracy?"

"Think bigger, Kyla."

"Common good?"

"Why would a man care anything for the common good of another man that he doesn't know or who is not in that man's family?" He swallowed while raising a brow.

I paused with no words to add.

"When was the first time in human history that the human race started caring about the lesser ones among them? Romans said they wanted to move into Germania because the people there were barbarian and threatened whose way of life?"

"The Roman's. Battles have always been about land acquisition or safety of your own people. What about it?"

"And every Roman citizen was on board with it, right?"

"Pretty much."

"Now, look at our wars in present day."

"Ok."

"The Iraq war. You were told it was to squash the terrorist, or our present day barbarians, in their home country. No different than this battle, right?"

"Right, but..." I played along but had no idea what he was getting at.

"Before that, would your American brethren have gone to war against people in another country far away from your home just for oil?"

"Oil? No. We're not like that. It took us being enraged and scared because of 9/11 for us to want or support a war in Iraq." Pictures of those buildings falling and all the devastation circled through my head.

"There were so many reasons why America wanted to go to war in Iraq, just one or two were revealed to you at the time. The rise of heroin in that area being one. I bet you didn't hear about that. There is so much more involved in these wars than you know."

I shifted my feet and agreed. "No. We were all focused on what happened in New York City."

"Why do we see land conquest as cruel now?"

I knew I looked confused.

"Yea well during this century, the Romans didn't have to play politics, they just did what they wanted. There was no 'love one another the way I love you'."

"You're quoting Jesus," I said confounded. I didn't think he was sure just yet of what was going on. It was more like he was thinking out loud to better process his thoughts.

"Listen, we don't have much more time, and I'm not sure I'm fully right about this. But I feel things are happening this way for a reason."

"Can you tell me how I can get you out?"

"Kyla, I don't know if that is in the cards for me. I'm being sold as a slave. No more under the radar for me."

I took in a deep breath and tried not to let my eyes tear up.

He leaned forward. "Are you alright?"

"Yeah, just go on." I played with the hem of my gown to distract myself.

He continued on, "So Emperor Augustus just wants to make sure the savages don't affect his kingdom or his advances in growing Rome's territory. And the Battle of Teutoburg Forest was the biggest battle in Roman history because it was the battle that stopped Rome from growing farther."

He paused and continued on with a sense of urgency. "Kyla, remember this is all just a theory based on what I've been gathering and what I've learned. You need to understand that the loss of this Battle of Tetoburg Forest was the first time the 'wind had been taken from Rome's sails', as you American's put it. In other words, this was the first time they lost a battle and didn't retaliate back stronger and continue on with their expansion into that said region. They had lost many before that but still came back years or so later to take the area and assimilate its people. After this battle, there were no more conquests for Rome anywhere. They officially stopped at the Rhine River and every other front around the entire empire. A regression of territory for the biggest super power the world has ever known began at this pivotal point in history and continued until 500 or so A.D. when Rome finally ceased to exist."

"So what does Parker want to do, help the Roman's win? Do you think we'd have a Roman empire still around in our time? No way. Eventually they would have fallen. It's inevitable."

"Is it? To change the way the dominos fall, Kyla, that's what Parker said. I believe, it was a foreshadowing or at least a hint of what is to come. I believe that him convincing the Senator to marry you off as a trade to the Germanic tribes and working with the Roman key players of that battle, points to him wanting to affect that battle in some way. I just don't know how yet."

"I don't follow." I stood up to look out from his cage.

"It didn't matter when Parker traveled back in time as long as he was able to effect one battle for one great empire and then everything would change. But this one. This one battle is set at the same time as the beginning of the end for Rome and the birth of the Christian faith. You can't say that that is a coincidence. And you will end up right in the middle of it all when this ship docks. You have a better chance than we ever had to make sure events stay the way history wrote them. That is why I'm telling you all this now."

"I don't know. What can one measly woman do, especially in these times?"

At that moment, we heard one of the legionnaires usher in. And I ran back to hold Eriksen. Dang, why did our last moments have to be spent debating history and battles? He took my face in his hands. "Look at me."

"Time to go," said Nero.

"Wait, one more second, please!" I spouted back.

"Look at me, Kyla." Eriksen emotionally got out. "This is the end of the mission for me and maybe the last time I can talk to you. I need you to hear something."

I looked up at him with teary eyes that I couldn't hold back and shook my head slightly. He glanced at the soldiers and then back at me with a smile like we weren't in that cell. Like he wasn't chained up and beaten. Like we were back at home. Our home, our time. "I came up to your office that night after we met on the elevator."

"What are you talking about? Back at West Bank Labs?" I whispered back even though speaking in English would not be understood by the legionnaires anyway.

"Yes. I found out who you were and where your office was. I don't know why I went up there. I guess I was... I don't know. We had just been briefed that afternoon about this mission and knew it was a one-way trip. I guess before I fully committed to leaving my time or even my son, I wanted to see you."

I looked at him with shock. "What?"

"I knew I needed to do this mission for the safety of my son and his future, but I guess I was hoping..."

"Hoping, what?"

"Hoping you would have looked up at me and given me a reason to stay."

"That's bull. Don't blame me for this! You never came to my office!"

"I did. I told you hi. And asked how you were?" he smiled at me again. "You were so staunchly involved in your work that you didn't even look up. You just said, 'good night' in that sweet, yet business voice, you have. So I just said, 'good night' back."

Awareness hit and I began crying harder. I shook my head as I started to have a recollection of that night. "I remember telling people goodnight. I do that every night though because I'm always staying late. I just never take the time to acknowledge anyone, you know?" I paused with wide eyes. "What have I done?"

"You've done what needed to be done. Because now I am here and so are you. Kyla, I don't believe in coincidences." He kissed my forehead and then touched his forehead to mine. "I need you to be focused on the mission like you were focused on that job back at the labs. You have the perfect opportunity to end this, and you are the best person to do it. I really believe that. I believe in you."

"NO! Stop! I just want to stay with you!"

He grabbed my head and pushed it to his chest breathing hard. "And I with you, but this is bigger than us, Kyla. Please, you have to do this. Everyone we ever loved is depending on us. I need you to stay strong."

Stopping with an intensity in his eyes that I've never seen before, he reached around his bloodied neck and unclamped his small crucifix necklace. Then against my wishes, he clamped the chain around my neck. "No, no, keep it. You need this. If things go bad at the games, you will need this more than me, please."

Then, the legionnaires decided to no longer wait patiently and grabbed my arm to pull me up and out of the cell. I grabbed to hold the charm on the necklace and noticed it too was dripping with Eriksen's blood. "No, please. Eriksen! No!" I fought with the soldiers so I could run back to touch him one more time, but they were too strong. They dragged me out of the cell screaming.

I couldn't believe we were here like this; him possibly facing death again and me facing a marriage to a stranger in another time. This didn't happen in our world. We weren't prepared or raised with this perspective of life. I began to choke and my heart started racing so fast I knew an anxiety attack was imminent. As I began to heave uncontrollably, I looked back to see Eriksen surprisingly so remarkably controlled. Disturbingly to me, he still had a look of peace on his face. Almost like he was happy. Like he knew everything would be okay.

"Remember Kyla, I don't believe in coincidences. I believe in something more."

And at that moment, I stood straight up, held my head high, and knew what I needed to do. Or thought I did. If anything, I just wanted to show Eriksen that I wouldn't let him down. I didn't want to leave him with the last emotion that he sees on my face to be one of fear. I wanted to show him 'hope' like he was showing on his face as he sat in that dreaded cell awaiting his possible end when the ship docked. Hope. Hope like that bird, that Phoenix thing, he referenced to back at the gardens that warm romantic night. That night that I first saw him for more than just a soldier, unbeknownst to him or me then. The night I realized he was protecting me because he cared for me all along. Foolish me so caught up in everything else that I didn't notice him. But I did that night and more so now. But that night was the night that I first fell in love with him.

Chapter 12

The next few days were a blur. I cried, slept, and then cried again. Malum tried to cheer me up on deck when he was off duty. But it didn't work. Even Tate's good humor wasn't enough anymore. So many things were running through my mind. I worried about Eriksen most of all. Aida would speak with me from time to time to keep me company too and tell me of our arrival in Venice, Italy. She and Malum also kept me apprised on Eriksen. My agreeing to this marriage afforded me the chance to save Eriksen before, but not in the games that were planned for next week there in Venice. After that vulgar exhibition, I would then be married and traveling to an even worse place than I had been in for the whole trip.

The Germanic people lived similar to how our American Indians did before Europeans, innovation, and running water. I would live on the land, hunt, and have babies. Ugh... the anxiety started to build again. Not only because it was such a desolate life compared my life in the city, but also because I had to lay with a man I did not know or love.

No matter how hard I tried, I couldn't shake the idea of running away or dying. If Eriksen died in the arena, I didn't know if I could go on. I didn't even know how I could help with the mission. I hadn't seen or heard from Banks and the others. Did they abandon us and forsake the mission? Were they even alive? I knew Parker would be with the Senator at the wedding, but would I be able to kill him and stop whatever he was planning? It was too much. Too overwhelming.

When we first arrived in Venice, I said my goodbyes to my new Phoenician friends and thanked God for solid ground. It was hard to look at Malum as we left the boat. He seemed so sad. I knew he would miss me more than most. I told him that one day he would meet a woman like me. That his day was coming. I even kissed him on the cheek after I hugged him.

I was later brought to Aida's villa where she tried to comfort me by saying the games were not always a fight to the death. And that many of the fights were staged for the crowd's benefit. Oh like our present day WWE, I think not. She said she would not be in attendance since she was an aristocrat, and her family would be frowned upon if she was seen there. But that the Senator would allow me to attend with a legionnaire escort and a slave by the name of Dias. I wanted badly to attend. I hadn't been able to see Eriksen since that day on the ship. Deep down I badly wanted to see him. Today was the day I'd at least get to, but at a distance. Even if it was just a few short minutes before he's slaughtered. Oh God, I couldn't think like that.

Mid afternoon, Dias and I were escorted from Aida's family villa in the heart of Venice to the city's amphitheater not far down the street. I had only seen things like this in the movies. I didn't realize how crazy these people were. What a paradox because for a society that claimed to be so civilized, they were far from it. People all around me were screaming when I got to my seat. I saw nicely dressed women and kids piled onto stone steps one on top of the other. I viewed grown men making foul gestures to each other paying no mind to the children around them. It was worse than Super Bowl SLIX between the New England Patriots and the Seattle Seahawks when Tom Brady took a knee close to the end of the game. You would have thought it was the end of the world. Both teams started fighting and people in the stands went crazy. Thankfully, no one died. But the way these Romans were acting here, I would have bet my bottom dollar that someone, other than the participants in the arena, would be dying sooner than later.

A finely dressed robust and bald man came out and announced the names of the famous three gladiators. The crowd went wild. As the men entered the arena, they were surprisingly over weight. I figured they would look different. Dias, tried to keep me abreast on everything in broken Latin. She was a slave from Cyprus, an island South of Macedonia in the Mediterranean Sea. She hated Romans and the games. However, she attended still. I figured out the birth of her angst came because her brother died by the hand of a gladiator just a year ago.

Then, the bald man announced that the opponents were slaves from all over Rome's great territories. He said they will be presented as Retiaruis and Myrmillonis warriors. Dias laughed. I frowned at her. "What's so funny?"

"The seasoned gladiators are performing as a Gallus with a gladius."

"And?"

"Gallus' have long swords. The slaves will wield short swords or even just knives. But they will have shields. Not sure what good that will do."

My heart sank as I watched the slaves walk out onto the field carrying exactly what Dias said. The crowd did not cheer for them. In the back of the six men, was Eriksen. He stood taller than the others, so he was easy to single out. He looked a lot better than he did on the ship. He must have been fed good and have rested well since getting to Italy.

All the competitors were dressed in just pants with their chests bare. Eriksen also was easy to spot because of his whiter skin where his shirt had protected him from the sun most of his life. And then there were the tattoos. The big one encompassing most of his right forearm was easily visible. I couldn't see the one on his back as much.

When the announcer gave the signal, the men started to come together. Two of the slaves ran back behind Eriksen, but he kept moving forward. He watched a few of the slaves face off with the gladiators and looked to be taking it all in. When he appeared ready, he flipped the dagger in his hand and plowed forward with a purpose. His shield was lifted high and his stance resembled that of a man on a mission. No pun intended.

One of the slaves that fought first, managed a blow to the first gladiator's leg. But then was stabbed in the cheek the second he drew up. I flinched as the blood sprayed out. The small slave managed to fight back still and thrust his knife into the side of the gladiator's neck. It looked like a kill shot. However, the Romans sent four men out to grab the wounded gladiator and pull him to safety. Dias said there would be no death for the celebrities.

While my attention was on that action, two slaves were killed rather violently. The smaller dark skinned one was stabbed in the chest, and the black headed one had tripped leaving him an easy target to his aggressor. He was screaming when the blade went into his breast. It was so hard to watch. That left Eriksen and the wounded slave alone with the last remaining gladiators.

Eriksen and the biggest gladiator came down on each other. It all went so fast that I couldn't tell what was happening. It seemed like more of a wrestling event. They blocked each other's sword thrusts with their shields and swung erratically trying to take first blood. Before I could register if there was a hit, they were both on the ground rolling around swinging. I couldn't take it, I stood and screamed. Dias grabbed my hand to pull me down. "Calm down, there hasn't been a major blow yet."

"How can you tell?"

"You can tell in how they move. Oh wait! Someone's hurt." And the crowd roared. The third gladiator was victorious over his own slave leaving the man hurt and possibly dying from an abdomen wound. Then, he approached Eriksen too. Two on one, I couldn't take it.

Eriksen managed to dodge the blows from his first opponent using his shield more as a weapon swinging it against the incoming sword. He appeared to be waiting on just the right moment. From behind came the third gladiator, and Eriksen dropped and rolled to the ground out of the way to do a quick maneuver up in time to block that sword. The crowd roared with excitement. They were getting quite a show.

As both gladiators were side by side heading Eriksen's way, Eriksen dodged an advance but couldn't move quick enough for the second. The third gladiator's sword drove right into his left shoulder, causing him to drop his shield and bend forward in pain. The crowd got to their feet with excitement, and I hated them for it.

Suddenly, the injured slave jumped up from behind the gladiator who just drew blood and shoved his dagger into the head of the unsuspecting man. In an effort to survive, that gladiator swung around and knocked the slave down with a solid blow to his chest. But the momentum left the gladiator stumbling till he fell on top of the slave. The audience actually laughed in amusement.

Eriksen had used the split second distraction to run back, grab his shield, and painfully block more blows from the second or last gladiator. He was injured pretty bad. So much that it weakened his arm to the point that he dropped the shield again. As I saw him curse out of frustration, the same four men that pulled the first gladiator out, came running out for the slave's fallen gladiator. "I can't believe it, that slave pummeled Venice's favorite gladiator." Dias said with wide eyes.

The crowd booed, and the last surviving gladiator, enthralled by the crowds, advanced on Eriksen again. Eriksen took a step or two back to get his bearings. He was calm and fierce. I had never seen anything like it. He spit to the side and prepared for the next attack. But he didn't have a sword or anything now, nor did he have time to rush over and get another one. Dread filled my belly. I held my breath.

This final gladiator stood slightly taller than Eriksen and quickly swung his sword at Eriksen's head. "That gladiator has a height and reach advantage over that blonde slave."

"Shhh," I told Dias.

Eriksen dodged the man's sword and kicked fast and hard enough knocking the sword out of the gladiator's hand. Without a moment's hesitation, he picked up his shield again to shove it into the gladiator. The gladiator fell back but regained balance. With what looked like sheer adrenaline, Eriksen came alive and rammed right into the gladiator sending him to the ground. The dust from the dirt drifted all around them to where I couldn't see the impact or what happened next. All I saw was the gladiator back with his sword and Eriksen gained one again too, presumably from the third gladiator.

They both circled each other waiting on the first to move. Eriksen looked badly wounded, but I stayed optimistic. "Come on Eriksen. Come on," I said quietly.

The modern day soldier didn't seem distracted by the crowd or the bloodshed. He was focused on killing. Like a wolf about to pounce on its prey. He looked to be someone that was just all out scary and trained to win. The gladiator returned the fierceness with a hateful expression. He wasn't as wounded but seemed to be growing tired. But the opposition did handle the sword more comfortably. Therefore, I knew Eriksen's best choice was to dodge the weapon as much as he could till the gladiator grew tired.

Eriksen did just that. Dodge after dodge with quick feet that I attributed to his martial arts training. Finally, the gladiator slowed down. Then, when I thought it was almost over for good, the gladiator got another strike in and wounded Eriksen on the leg. My hand flew to my mouth, and I decided I couldn't watch anymore. I turned away as Dias screamed and the crowd went silent. "What, what happened? No, don't tell me."

Dias turned to me. "I can't believe it. The slave killed him."

I immediately swung back around to see the arena. Eriksen was sitting on the ground with his arms around his knees. He looked tired and shocked. When the Romans came to collect their gladiator, Eriksen stood up and stumbled backward with his empty hands in the air as if to say, "I'm done. Not a threat." They dragged their fighter off with what looked like a mortal wound to his chest.

"Oh my goodness, how?" I said excitedly.

"The slave did some kind of kick that pushed the gladiator's sword to the side. It gave the slave enough time to sneak in and strike at the chest." She was half excited herself, though she would never admit that she was glad the slaves won this one.

The crowd was quiet for a minute or so, and then raised to their feet in applause. Eriksen just stood there shocked and not knowing what to do. I smiled with a beaming smile of pride at my hero. I couldn't believe it myself.

"Next time, he won't be so lucky. He's good but not that good. It was just a good day." Dias said while clapping with the crowd.

****

A few hours later after another battle began between animals and volunteer fighters, Dias was ready to leave. She said that since the main event was over, there was no use hanging around. I didn't want to leave. I guess I was hoping I'd get another glance at Eriksen maybe coming around on the field, or something. I didn't know, I just wanted to see him. Then, she said what sounded like music to my ears. "You know we can go down and see the fighters?"

"What?"

"Down in the pits." She stood and moved toward our escort to have a word. When she came back, she told me, "He approved. But just for a few minutes and then back to the villa."

I couldn't believe it. But then again, the Senator did say I could see him after the game, if he lived. And he did!

We walked down the gloomy steps similar to four flights of stairs, and into a dark chamber lined with four alcoves on both sides. It was lit with candles all along the walls. Dias led the way with a defiant swing of her hips and pointed at each alcove. When we got to the middle set, I noticed several women down by one room, a barred holding cage. It was Eriksen they were wooing over, and he looked like a Cheshire cat because of it.

The women were beautiful and model tall. Probably Venice's finest that snuck down here to get a peek of this slave turned celebrity. A man from a different time who miraculously beat a seasoned gladiator. One woman let down her blonde hair as if to stimulate the hero. She giggled and smiled at him in a floosy way. I grew sick to my stomach.

Right then, he noticed me and stood up while holding a big bandage on his shoulder. The women turned to glimpse at what caught his interest and frowned at me. "You can go ladies," he said sternly dismissing them in perfect Latin. One by one they ambled on by me fighting their pride like upset roosters.

I got closer to the door of the cage and did not say a word. He came closer to the gate to get within inches of me. "Hello," he said, his face beaming.

"Yea, hey. Was I interrupting something?" I asked, but I couldn't mute my heightened senses.

"Now what do you think?"

"They were basically going to strip for you, Eriksen."

"And?" he asked with another grin he couldn't contain.

"I bet you like that."

"Come on Kyla, I've been around women like that my whole adult life. Groupies pinning for the hero. They don't do it for me anymore."

"It didn't look that way."

"Give me a break. I thought I was dead today. And God I'm glad to see you." He put his hands on the bars separating us.

Being stubborn I struck back. "Yeah well, I'm an engaged woman, remember?"

He swallowed hard. Then, his shoulders sagged, and I saw a flash of a pained stare. The poor guy was full of sweat, blood, and dirt. But I would have given anything to be able to go into that cage with him like those women were trying to do. Shame on me, but it crossed my mind.

Dias walked up and urged me to go. Our escort was coming and we were out of time. That was when my own foolish pride fell apart, and I grabbed at his hands through the wires. "I'm sorry. I'm just worked up."

"From my amazing fight?" he asked shyly. But he didn't hide his inner pride.

"Shut up, Mr. Jolly, and be serious. I still haven't seen Parker or know anything new. When are you supposed to fight again?"

"It's several days of fighting. I go out again in three."

"I'm supposed to be married in two. By the time you fight again, I'll be gone."

My escort soldier walked up and grabbed my arm forcefully. Eriksen dropped his calm demeanor and gave the young soldier a 'go to hell' look. "Time to go woman," the boy responded while wearily looking toward Eriksen.

I bit my lip and forced him to look my way. "Eriksen, please promise me something."

"What?"

"Win one more to give me more time."

He nodded his head, but I knew his body was too weak for another round in three days. But we made it this far. With the odds stacked against us, we made it. Modern day people hanging in there in an ancient world.

I gently kissed his hand through the bars and fixed my posture upright like an aristocrat myself. Walking away from him again was not an easy feat.

Chapter 13

The scintillating sun was radiating its morning rays through the glass paned windows in my dream. I was experiencing my 'River Dream' again. And in that dream, I had been highly anticipating the coming days. However, I couldn't figure out why. And even though I was excited about what was to come, I still harbored a faint feeling of weariness and loneliness. A feeling of dread and regret.

The front door came open causing the Indian decorated bells hanging above it to give off their high pitched warning. Doses of the sultry heat and noise pollution from the boardwalk trolley outside spilled into the bayou room. I was then distracted from my foolish daze by a tall figure dressed in rugged clothes and muddy boots. I was quite aggravated by his presence that I didn't even look back up when I spoke to him. The man smiled my way and waited patiently by the door until I was ready. Ready for what? I couldn't figure it out. There was just something I knew I was going to do for him. Something important to him but not yet pertinent for me.

When I finally decided to give him all my attention, I woke up. I still couldn't recall what the mystery man looked like. Young or old, or what. I just remembered his presence like I did when I woke from that dream the last time I had it back in high school. Back on the tear-soaked bank of the Mississippi River. I remembered it like a kind, warm energy that came over me when he appeared. Sadly, what stuck were the beautiful surface feelings from it, but not many more details. Was the man, Eriksen? Either way, I wanted to go back to sleep and fall into that dream again.

But no, I had to wake up. It was the morning of judgment day, as I called it. Aida and Viggo came in to tell me of the tribe's arrival in Venice. The tribe leaders were first meeting with Jacobus, Jacobus's commander, and the Senator to solidify their tentative agreement. A lot of which included me as a bride to their prince along with some priceless trades from Asia.

Aida took my hands and sat with me on the bed's velvety red duvet. She wrinkled her brow and squeezed my fingers into her palms. "Today, it is very important that you look presentable and beautiful. If the tribe leader does not like what he sees, everything could fall apart."

"I don't care. I can't do it Aida." By not being any help to Eriksen or the mission yet and *still* fearing his impending death, I had no will left in me.

Aida leaned forward, her eyes cold and flinty. "Kyla, you listen to me. I don't fully know where you and your men came from. But what I do know is that this is how things are done here. Here in Rome. Honestly, you shock me with your stubbornness."

"Excuse me?"

"If the tribal leader does not take to you or you ruin this in anyway, these conspirators will kill Eriksen before he even gets another chance to battle. Slaughtered while helpless in his sleep. There is still so much at stake. Honor him with your courage now at this important hour in both of your lives. Honor him in a way only a strong woman can. The type of woman he thought *you* were."

"Aida, he's dead anyway. There is no way he'll survive a second round. He has severe injuries. He can't possibly..."

Her ivory hand went up. "At least he'll have a fighting chance. And you underestimate that man still. There is something so cunning in the way he handles himself in person and in that arena. He is extremely smart and extremely dangerous."

She admired Eriksen. I could tell in the way her eyes gleamed when she spoke of him like a mother does of her child. "Oh God, I wish you knew everything. You wouldn't be so certain." *Tap, tap*. I looked toward the door. Viggo stepped closer and grabbed my hands to give me a small kiss on my knuckles. He was saying goodbye. Then, they left as a new stranger walked in.

"Important day today," she told me. I watched the new servant come through the door wearing only a small wrap over her chest and one around her bottom section. It was very similar to a bikini and very distasteful. "My name is Cassius. My master bids me to make sure you are alluring to his guests."

That explained it. She was the Senator's slave. Of course he would have his woman dressed so provocatively. The vermin probably took liberties with the poor girl. She was very pretty. She had a lithe body, a sweet heart-shaped face with green eyes, and long medium blonde hair. She acted like it was the norm to walk around dressed like she was. She had learned to endure her predicament.

She helped me into a fine linen gown of dainty white with subtle embroidered flowers surrounding the bodice. So small, you could hardly make out their form without close examination. The dress was belted with a special knot that Cassius called 'the knot of Hercules'. When I rolled my eyes she said, "Only your husband can remove it."

My hair was left down to show off all my unique qualities, as the Senator required. However, it was brushed back and adorned with a Roman gold and feathery hair pin to the left side of my face. Cassius, proud of her work, showed me my image in a small mirror. "What do you think?" Her almost translucent skin glowed with pride.

"I guess it will have to do for my dreaded wedding day," I said with my heart thudding dully in my chest.

The porcelain doll before me flushed. "You are fortunate. The barbarian prince is *very* desirable. A bit hairy but still very appealing. He is of my people."

"You are a Chatti?"

"No. My tribe was the Cananefates, but most of us were slaughtered during the first war. My parents and brothers were burned in front of me." She stopped and stared down at her still hands. Her next words came slow and steady. "That was when I was taken as a Roman slave. I was sold three times before I made it here." When her voice cracked, she rose to hide her emotions and gently took back the mirror from me.

"I'm sorry." I seemed to be saying that a lot.

She gave me a half-shrug. "I don't remember much. I was a wee one."

I didn't believe her, but smiled with understanding anyway. "Do you like it here in Venice?"

"I do. It is a nice place. I have met many good people here." She paused and looked at me. "You will like it back in Germania, though. To be among the trees and open air. To have nothing better to do than sit among the chirping birds and listen to the stream trickle by as it drifts across the rocks."

I studied her crestfallen face. "It sounds lovely."

She smiled and every tooth was nicely aligned. "You will love it."

I felt for her and for me. We talked for awhile about Rome and Germania. It helped to have someone to talk to while waiting on the event that I dreaded with my whole being. I enjoyed talking with Cassius. In just a short amount of time, I felt she could have been a close friend to me in these times, and if I would have been able to stay in Venice.

****

The barbarian tribe came in a little while later to evaluate their prize. I was harshly warned to keep my mouth shut by Jacobus. The room warmed up as I was presented for display like a slave to be sold. I held my head up high and did not make eye contact. The five men of the Chatti tribe walked in proudly with the Roman liaison, Atticus, following behind. The Chatti, burly men appeared relaxed and were dressed very similar to each other with a plain tunic and tartan strung over one shoulder. All were tall and had worn faces presumably caused from the elements. Not a single one was without a scruffy beard around their jaws and upper lips, as well as tattoos on their hands and necks.

The oldest stared at me frowning. Then, he asked Atticus, "Why is she so small? How would it be possible a union of breeding with such a delicate thing?" He lifted his sword hand toward me.

Atticus answered in the German's native tongue, "She is a Roman with Jewish blood. The Jewish women produce many offspring each. You will not be disappointed. She is also very intelligent and so will be her children."

The German's voice lowered. "Hmm...Jewish? I have never seen a Jewish woman, but she is a beauty." He peered at me closely, and I shivered inside as his foul breath reached my face. "Aged twenty, correct?"

"Of course," Atticus replied. I grimaced because that age was a little off. However, I knew I would pass because women aged more quickly in this time.

Then, the leader grabbed my face to force my mouth open. "These teeth!

She does have good genes." He smiled and stepped back to allow what I presumed was his son move toward me.

In no time, the younger man erased the distance between us. He faced me straight on with a smile building on his angular face. The guy's eyes were blue too but wider and darker than Eriksen's. He had freckles all over his face and a huge scar under his left eye. His lips were thin and for the most part, he was not unruly. He just needed a better bath and more care to his wild shoulder length hair. My mind screamed lice, but I squashed it to keep my composure. The warrior prince spoke with a softer, yet authoritative voice. "Woman, my name is Gerhard Naharvali Gutes of the Chatti tribe. I *will* take thee as my wife." He smiled menacingly and turned back to his men to share a moment of laughter with his clan.

Gerhard's broad shoulders reminded me of Eriksen too, but his beard and face were similar to his father's with their rough-hewn features. Gerhard looked more like a forty-year-old to me, but I assumed he was in his twenties. Possibly even closer to my real age. I nodded shakily and lifted my chin back up.

My mind was racing as I thought of this man and me together every day for the rest of my life. I would do my duties for the years to come to stay alive. But at night, I would dream of Eriksen to keep my heart intact. I would see Eriksen's soft eyes when Gerhard's lust for me needed to be quenched. I would feel Eriksen's hands when Gerhard's touch encompassed me. That was how I would survive. I hated this place. I wanted to go home. I sunk my thumb nail into my palm to distract me and keep me from crying.

They wasted no time leaving and proceeding on with their other dealings. I let out the breath I was holding as soon as they left the room and slumped down to the cold floor. My dress gathered at my folded legs. That exchange revealed that I would in fact be marrying that man in less than six hours. Marrying. The 'M' word. Something I never spoke of before, but now I was being forced into one with a true brute. One that put my first ever thoughts of Eriksen to shame.

****

Thud, thud, thud. I wiped my tears and saw the door to my room open shortly after the third knock. I think I cried for over two hours. I was thirsty and tired again. Hoping that my next guest was the sweet Cassius, I stood with a smile. But in walked Parker!

He came in with an all-business look and carried a small bag wrapped in a deep blue blanket.

The smug looking man summoned the guards to tie me up to a chair before they made their leave, closed the door, and waited outside. The rope was tight around my wrists, and for the first time in this whole horrible ordeal, I felt like meat being traded and not a human being anymore. He didn't even look me in the eye when he walked in or while I was being tied up. I yanked at the rope while he pulled around a stool and sat directly in front of me addressing me for the first time. "Hello."

Sweat poured down my brow and the feeling of panic set in. I was trapped with this maniac and had no clue what he was planning to do to me. But to my shock, he knew and planned way more than we even imagined. Made obvious when he continued to address me. "Ms. Marshall, my name is Simon Parker and yes, I know who you are."

I held my tongue. We had been so careful. How did he know?

"Or at least I know someone close to you and that is how I came to know you."

"I don't understand."

He looked around the room for eavesdroppers but still spoke in English for ease. "You did work as a contractor for Stellar Solutions, did you not?"

Still no comment on my part as I debated the best way to handle his interrogation.

"I'll take that as a yes. Kyla Marshall, daughter of Sarah Marshall and Arye Horowitz. We know everything."

We? What?

"I worked with your father years back until he stole from us, and we never saw him again."

"You knew my father?"

He ignored my question and continued, "Imagine my shock when I see you walk in to that dining room in Tripoli. You should be back in the year two thousand seventeen running a useless campaign to help your clients. One that we knew would end soon."

"Who's we?"

Still he did not answer my questions. He kept asking his own. "Why are you here?" He peered at me for a moment with his strange hazel eyes and quirky expression. “Hmm. I know you will not tell me the truth anyhow and it doesn’t matter now. When I saw you, I knew what needed to be done. You were the perfect piece to the puzzle that I’ve needed to put together in order to achieve our goal. A woman of my time. Dangerous, extremely dangerous, in fact. Unless she was tied down and controlled. Not only did I need to get rid of you but also a woman like you is a perfect pawn in power play negotiations.”

“What goal?” I said seething through my teeth.

“Oh, you are just so innocent and naïve aren’t you? I bet you really believe in that whole democracy propaganda they filled your mind with back in America.” He stood up and moved back to the table where his bag lied. While rummaging through it, he said, “You see, America and the world is controlled by just a few people, my dear.”

“You’re talking one world government. That’s conspiracy theory talk.”

“Believe what you want, it doesn’t matter what you believe anyway.” He said while he pulled out a vial and syringe from his bag.

I froze and ascertained that I was in more trouble than just a mere marriage. I needed him to talk more. I needed to know what his intentions were. “So if I believe this theory of yours. What does that have to do with time travel and you?”

He prepped his tools and continued to speak with his back toward me. “Try this parable. Imagine you were in a family ran by a man and woman who agreed whole heartedly for years. Then all of the sudden, things changed. Something happens in their home that they didn’t see coming, and they were forced to evolve to handle it. What happens when one doesn’t want to evolve and disagrees with the other?” He looked back at me with a sly smile. “Before you say divorce, think more brutally, Kyla.”

He pushed the syringe into the vial and withdrew the clear substance up into the syringe. Then, he approached me. “You see, there are people with political powers bigger than your imagination. And they are not agreeing with each other anymore. Therefore, one group needs to wipe out the other. But in our time, it is virtually impossible anymore. However, in this time, or at least this far into the past, the skies the limits.” His unbalanced smile on hawk-like features made me flinch.

"What is that?" I lifted my chin toward what he had in his hand.

"This is the most important weapon I could ever bring. And the most nondescript one of all. It is the most dangerous virus of our time," he said with pride in his expression.

"Ebola?"

"No, not Ebola. Marburg, which is as fatal as Ebola."

"What is Marburg?"

"It is a hemorrhagic fever virus like Ebola. Its fatality rate is eighty-eight percent, close to Ebola's ninety percentage rate. Pretty impressive, isn't it?"

"That's a population ender in this time!" I became dizzy. His sinister smile was now getting blurry.

"Well yes, except for the chosen ones who are given the vaccine."

"How could it have a vaccine? Ebola doesn't even have a vaccine." I was fighting but bravery was losing.

"Actually, we have the vaccine for both."

"That figures. So who gets the bad doses?" I caught his arm swing behind my head out of the corner of my eye. He grabbed my arm from behind and stuck the syringe in my shoulder before I could react.

"You do." At the injection site, a warm, heavy fluid moved into my arm. He walked back to his bag before turning back to face me. "And now you are my Typhoid Mary, Ms. Marshall. Congratulations."

"What do you mean?" I began to shake. My bladder almost loosened.

"You will be contagious within forty-eight hours to maybe three days. Right around the time you get closer to reaching Magna Germania with your new husband and his family. There you will infect the Germanic people. In turn, it will cause them to loose the Battle of Teutoburg Forest which will make a huge alternate impact on the Roman Empire for the good. Think of the Aztec Indians from your part of the woods, Kyla. Weaken the enemy with a virus and then attack."

I shook my head slightly and held back the tears as the spot on my shoulder started to sting. However, I wasn't going to show fear.

"Now, Ms. Marshall just remember that you need a home here in this time. The Germanic people will be your best bet for that and safety until your passing. They are loyal people and the prince is quite smitten with you. Try to run from him and well, they are barbarians. Who knows what they would do to a deserter."

I couldn't gather my senses to understand what he was saying or to argue with him as he walked out the door. I was in trouble and didn't know what to do next. As I heard his footsteps move farther away down the hall. The sensation of things moving like wild horses made me sick. It was another panic attack brewing. I tried to take deep breaths to calm myself, but it was futile. I leaned over and vomited all over my tied up feet.

Chapter 14

Have you ever danced not knowing the proper steps, but you let the music and your partner lead you around the floor? You shuffle from side to side with the melody pulling your body around like a dirt devil on an unknown course that only the rhythm and rhyme would reveal. But you follow harmoniously. The soft caress of his touch and your will gone adrift, you feel the rush and take it all in. Your body is a beautiful, perfect, and erotic instrument held captive by the moment and the music. Such nice music, such a nice escape.

But the music grew softer and softer until it was only a humming in my ears as I was presented to the crowd just a few hours later. A man to my left held my hand and walked me toward an organic aisle of beaten down grass leading to an arched wall. It was set between two columns with a raised alter reflecting the day's last rays of light.

At the end, or my final destination, stood several German men laughing and drinking as if it were a party and not my funeral. The officiant must have been the temple priest seeing how he was fully robed in deep purple and gold tassels. Standing not too far from him but off to the right, I could make out Senator Nicator, Decurion Jacobus with some of his legion, and Parker.

My mind and vision were spotty and confused. I couldn't tell you how I walked even a few steps. But I did so with a grace that didn't come from me. But a grace that was comforting and steady in a way that helped me glide a few more steps. The crowd of people around me smiled and cheered, though I knew not a single one. I just kept my eyes forward and continued to comfort myself with the faux music playing softly in my head.

When shock takes hold, you move on autopilot like it's a dream. And I did just that till halfway down the aisle. I was cognizant enough to know that it was not a dream and I was not imagining a child crying. I paused to see and noticed a little one, that had been positioned at her mother's feet, screaming upward to be held. To be held and comforted. I stopped and did not take another step. I thought of where I had come from, my childhood, my mistakes, and my life in this time. Also of my heartaches and the way I wasted precious time. So much time gone on a career that brought me nothing but loneliness. And now I am to die and take down others with me, possibly including this child.

I looked down to my feet willing them to move. My body began to shake. I wouldn't be able to stand it if I infected anyone. A tear slid down my cheek as I knew I had no hope left in my heart. And then I noticed it. Tucked below the neckline of my gown, the necklace Eriksen gave me when I saw him locked in that cage on the Phoenician ship. I pulled it out of my gown to hold it. On it, I viewed a figure of a man, his head leaned over to one shoulder, and his face carrying the burden of sadness. Sadness for whom? Why did he die?

I swallowed slowly and settled my eyes up to the sky. This man died to give us hope. Hope and a new start. The clouds in my mind lifted, and I could see something I had never seen before. I could see it in my childhood tucked away barely shining through on special, happy days. I could see it when my friends came to help me weather my darkest times. I could see it in that Roman cell when Eriksen's face showed calm as I faltered hard in fear.

I finally, at that moment, saw it in myself. I saw peace. Peace that brought me courage that I had never had before. Courage that wasn't orchestrated for a self-serving purpose. But courage that came freely and uninhibited and out of my whole being. As a smile moved across my face, I knew I was finally not alone. There was someone with me. I knew what I needed to do.

I dropped to my knees and heard the crowd quiet in awe. I bowed my head to the metal charm that reminded me of what I had forgotten. This picture depicting a faith that I never took serious until then. I did the sign of the cross that was taught to me by my mother, but that my father would turn away from. Then, I peered up at everyone around me, Romans, Germans, and Jews, most of which practiced polytheism. All were following my movements in disbelief. I had that one chance to convince them that they needed to stop me from moving on. To kill me before I infected everyone and changed the world to the worse.

I heard a man beside me speak angrily, "What are you doing?"

I lifted my chin high and spoke as bold and loud as I could so everyone could hear. "In the not too distant future a man will walk among you." I smiled bigger as more and more became clear. "He was born in the freezing cold and is living poorer than the poorest among you. But He will be the King of all kings though He will not want jewels, empires, land, or power. He will come just to help us. To help us learn peace, love, and happiness without fighting, conquering, and persecuting others. And He will do this in a way that will include everyone, not just Jews, but Egyptians, Germans, and all... It will be because of Him that you, Romans, will also be accepted and shown the way too. The way to Him. The way to the one *true* God."

And with absolute ruthlessness, I added while looking around, "There is only *one* God!"

Finally, there was movement from the guards ahead, and after a few minutes, Decurian Jacobus moved forward. "This woman speaks not for the empire. She speaks blasphemy against our gods. She will be put to death, as well as you!" He pointed to the scientist, Parker. "It was you who advised us to offer this evil one to our friends. You have brought this chaos upon us. You will suffer for your betrayal of Rome."

Oddly, Haman Parker did not look upset when the tall legionnaire went up behind him and thrust his sword in through his back and pierced his heart. The long blade then protruded out from his chest. Blood spread all over the front of his taupe robe.

I gasped and lowered my eyes to the ground. I knew it was now my turn. Thankfully, I at least lived to see the mission almost complete. All that was left was finishing off *me*. And *then* we would have succeeded.

The sand and rocks below me were suddenly miles away. I was mentally drifting above the ground. A young soldier appeared by my side grounding my body back down as I noticed his sword lifting up behind me. I knew they had to do this now to make an example out of me so no one would dare speak again like I spoke. But I had no choice. I told myself I would be fine as long as I kept my eyes locked on the gravel below my shaking knees.

Then I heard it. A light *thunk*, *thunk*. It sounded familiar but out of place.

I heard the sword drop to the ground and felt the young man brush beside me as he surprisingly fell to the earth next to his sword. A drip of blood ran from his chest. I knew instantly what that sound was.

I stood up watching the crowd react in shock and heard someone yell to me to run toward the hills. I took off in a sprint in that direction faster than I had ever ran before. And I could run. Four years of track in high school with several medals proved that. I had a furious endurance and when my muscle memory kicked in, I flew out of the assembly area like a hawk on the jet stream.

I dashed onto the street, thankfully my sandaled feet gained better traction. I heard the legionnaire give an order. Then, soldiers chased behind me through the crowds. I ran and ran breathing in the dirt off the street and dodging the bystanders and shops out in the courtyard. As I rounded the corner, I saw horses up the hill in the distance. Pushing my legs harder and harder, relief started coursing through my veins.

Suddenly, I heard men on cavalry horses rush around the corner. They pursued faster and faster. Then, they came up closer behind me bridging the gap. My legs began to weaken and I started to worry that I wouldn't make it. Just when the ground began to blow up dust at my heels from the hooves of the horses behind me, I heard *thump, thump* again and again. As I ran, I turned my head to look back as several men crumpled over and off their saddles. There was no doubt that it was a distance shot by a sniper rifle. I have never, ever loved a gun until that moment.

****

The top of the hill still seemed a mile a way. Stamina was never an issue for me in track, so I could keep running at a steady pace as long as I didn't have to sprint. With my last breath, I made it to the top of the hill expecting to see Eriksen, the sniper that saved me. Instead as I got closer, I saw Banks come up from behind one of the horses where he had secured the rifle. "Kyla, hurry get on!"

"Are we going back for Eriksen?"

"No, he's dead." Banks said as he walked up to help me to my horse.

I slumped down on the ground.

"We don't have time for this, Kyla. The Romans are going to sick the whole damn legion on us if you don't come on right now!"

I nodded and stood up. Wearily, I picked my foot up for him to help push me on to the horse. We took off on the blessed animals at a quick pace. We must have ridden for hours until he slowed down, and I finally could ask, "How did Eriksen die?"

"From his injuries in the game."

I dropped my head and warm tears ran down my face. Regret and anger swirled through my soul.

"One of them got infected, and it spread too quickly. Are you okay?" he asked sweetly.

"Why is everyone always asking me that? And how are you here?" I said wiping my face with the back of my hand.

"He didn't tell you?"

"Tell me what?"

"After Macedonia, he ordered us to hang back and keep a distance for the rest of the mission. He knew the Senator was up to something."

"Of course he did. He always planned ahead." I bit back more tears knowing that it explained why he was so forward with me on his return from Macedonia. He knew he may not have that chance again. So he made a move on me just to get one kiss? I shook the memory away so I could keep calm. "So how did you make it here to Venice?"

"Under your nose. Roberts and Toms too. They're meeting us at a rendezvous point up north of here."

"I thought y'all abandoned us?"

"That's not how soldiers work, Kyla. We never leave our own behind. And you're one of ours now."

"I didn't know that. And thank you. But what do you mean, under my nose?"

"It turns out the Phoenicians value gold *a lot*. All we had to do was offer them a few coins and they let us travel on their boat hidden as marines with our weapons in cargo. No questions asked. Good people those Phoenicians."

"You rowed the damn boat?"

"Yea, I thought for sure you'd notice us when you came down on the third or so day. We were in the back."

I don't know if it was Eriksen's death or the stress of the day, but I just started crying.

"Hey" he stopped the horses and moved me closer with his hand on my shoulder. "Just take a second. I know it's been a hard few days. I need you calm, so we can make it out of here."

I shook my head. "I know. Parker's dead too."

"I know. I saw through the scope. Are you okay now?"

"Yes, I'm fine." Dammit with all the commotion and adrenaline, I forgot that I wasn't fine. I'm infected! "Banks, wait!"

"We can't, we've got to keep moving?" he said agitated now.

"No, you don't understand. I can't keep going with you," I said adamantly.

"Like hell you can't."

I yanked from him and turned my horse to allow access for a quick get a way. "Stay away from me!"

"What the hell is going on?" he jumped down and reached for me and my horse taking the reins forcefully from me.

"Parker. He visited me right before the wedding. He had the virus." I pushed both hands into my hair. "I have the virus!"

"Great! Where? Give it to me."

I shook my head and my eyes flooded with tears again. It wasn't my finest hour. "It's in me. He injected it into me." I jabbed a finger at my left shoulder in agitation.

He paused and didn't know what to say.

"You weren't supposed to save me. I was supposed to die so no one else would get infected."

Banks shook his head. Concern passed across his usually boyish face. "Nope, no, not how it's going down."

"I'll just ride off somewhere away from everyone. You go before I'm contagious. I have maybe a day or so until I start to shed the virus." I was pleading with all the energy I had left.

Banks inhaled deeply through his nose, then exhaled slowly. "I'm not leaving you. I promised him I would get you somewhere safe. And that safe place is not much farther away. Come on Kyla, they are waiting for us in Reatia close to Germania."

"Parker wanted me to spread the virus around the Germanic people. If I go there, he will have won."

"We'll discuss it all later. I'm not leaving without you. I told my brother I'd get you there safely. If you don't go, I stay here and die with you." He crept closer to me. "Come on."

"You don't know what you're doing?" I told him.

"Honey, I've been through worse."

He got back on his horse with a glib expression. "Heck, I wasn't going to let that freak of long shot that saved you go unnoticed. I'm looking forward to bragging about that shot. You know, being that I'm not the gifted sniper that Eriksen is."

I laughed slightly at the humor. It helped settle my nerves. "So how do you know your way around out here?"

He reached under his garb and pulled out a compass. "I call her Pam. She's saved my life many a times in Boy Scouts." He put it back up. "Actually, all soldiers carry a compass. We brought most of our gear with us. And ancient maps. We're not stupid Kyla. We always do missions prepared." He smiled with those dimples. "And there are more things we snuck through from our time too."

"Like what?"

"Things."

I dropped it. "Oh. How long will it take us to get to Reatia?"

"It's an all day ride."

He signaled and off we went.

Chapter 15

I wanted to talk and learn more on the way, because Banks was always the one that filled me in on more things than the others. But I wasn't sure if I wanted to know anymore. What would it matter anyway? I'm going to be dead in a few days. And I'll be dying alone without Eriksen. Before night fall, we came up on a little village off the beaten path. Banks dismounted to talk to an older man walking a donkey. When he came back, he told me were were on the right track. A few more hours and we would be in Reatia.

The trip was taking a little longer than planned, but a few hours later, we were finally there. It was another tiny village.

Banks knew I was spent. He helped me dismount and walked me inside a straw hut where an old lady stood pointing to a small bed. The sweet soldier settled me in and walked out. Before I knew it, I was asleep from the exhaustion of the day.

I slept the rest of the night and into most of the next day. Every now and then I would hear voices in and out, but they managed to stay away from me. Banks must have told them. I decided I didn't care if I went back to sleep and slept my entire last days away.

Later in the day when the sun was starting to set, I awoke to the sound of several horses. I peeked up above my blanket and noticed my throat was sore. As I moved around the bed, I began shivering. My wedding gown, once the color of pearls, was covered in sweat and dirt. There was an argument breaking outside and I just knew I was being kicked out. I closed my eyes to block it all out when the door swung open and in walked someone I thought I'd never see again. Banks was following and yelling right behind him.

My feverish heart jumped. "Eriksen? It must be the virus making me hallucinate. You look like someone I know."

He dropped to the floor by me and took my hand. "It's me, Kyla."

"What?" I took in his furrowed brows and shook my head. "But Banks said you were dead."

"I told him to tell you that so you'd leave Venice. I knew you wouldn't if you thought I was alive and still trapped there."

"I don't get it. How did you get out?"

He had a gash above his eyebrow and a bandage wrapped around his bicep, but he smiled anyway. "We can make deals with the Germanic people too, Kyla. Everyone around here loves gold. And they especially loved the idea of how we could ambush the Romans. The Germans know that the Romans will still pursue their land. They're not stupid people."

"But Arminius does that?"

"He still will, they just don't know all the details yet. In fact, just as history wrote it, Arminius is already secretly meeting with the tribes while in and out of Germania."

"He's back in Rome now?"

"Yes, for now."

"So they got you out? How?"

"It wasn't real hard. We needed to first free you by sabotaging the wedding in some way. Banks waited for the right time. I heard how it went down, by the way." He said with another grin. "Then since the marriage didn't take place, the Germans asked to take back a prized gladiator instead for a trade. My men, Viggo, and Aida were already in talks with them, even before the wedding, to make sure it went according to plan."

"I thought Viggo and Aida betrayed us. Now that I think about it, it was Viggo that told me to run during my wedding procession," I added after thinking back.

"They never betrayed us. They were helping us even back in Tripoli. They are the ones who told my men what boat we were traveling on and all the other details when they saw what the Senator did."

"So you knew your men were on our ship?"

"Yea," he said half heartily.

I wanted to reach out and touch him but knew I couldn't. "So, I guess you heard?"

"Kyla, I'm so sorry. I never..."

I held up my hand. "Don't, you couldn't have known. But look at me. I walked among the enemy and got the inside scoop." I laid back with eyes to the roof when I began to feel faint. "Think of me like your Afghan war spy, Hamid Karzai. I was a prominent Roman for a little while. I am pretty proud of myself for working as a real agent, excluding getting a deadly virus. I was just glad that I could finally be of value to the team."

"You have always been a value to us." He felt my head and continued, "How do you know about Hamid Karzai?"

"Watched in a documentary one day in the dentist's office."

My heart unclenched at his laugh. "That's funny. I can see you sitting there bored and nothing else to do but watch war shows."

I turned back to him when my head eased up. "Yep. Anyway, Parker told me almost everything."

I spent the next few minutes relaying all that I learned about the two feuding world dynasties and the virus being their answer to wiping one out. Eriksen took it all in. He commented about how he was right to infer that the war in Germania was a target. The information strengthened his plan that the team should stay and make sure the war is still won by the Germans.

When I was done, I covered my face with my hands. "Promise me something."

"Yes, what is it?"

"Leave now and don't come back."

"I can't do that Kyla," he whispered next to me.

"I've started running a fever. I'm contagious now. I've told you everything you need to know, and I've gotten to see you. But now you need to go." I wasn't as brave as my words sounded. I just didn't want to see him get sick.

"No."

"You promised."

I glanced back at him and noticed his face contorted. "I'll leave the hut. But I'm not going far." He wiped his face while looking away and stood to leave. But he just ended up hovering above me, looking down at me.

To lighten the mood so he'd leave, I joked, "Remember, you are a pretty good gladiator after all."

"Yeah, but it didn't do you any good, did it?" And then he left.

The next few days, the only visitor I had was the elderly lady who would come in to bring me fresh water. She didn't come too close and didn't stay long. On the fourth day, I couldn't even acknowledge her presence. All I noticed when she left, was seeing Eriksen stand in the doorway to get a look at me.

The nausea came on quickly over and over, and I was sure I couldn't take anymore. On the fifth day, I lost control of most of my body that I couldn't keep my eyes open long enough to make out the sun through the window. I touched the crucifix on my neck and before I knew it, everything went pitch dark...

Chapter 16

Several more days had passed. Winter was at our door. I could feel the Artic booting up for the new season as the rest of the leaves lay waste on the frigid ground. The funny thing about these type of ops was that they gave you a chance to experience nature. To see God's design in the most rudimentary sense without the distraction of the television or computers. That was something positive about this job that guided my days among the negative that haunted my nights.

I made my way back to Kyla's hut and heard the news that I knew was coming. She had gone back to sleep for too long. She was probably not going to wake up again. It took everything I could do to not barge in there. To not take her hand and pull her close to me. I had watched so many of my friends die either at a distance or by my side. I could name every last one of them.

Michael Smith was the most recent. He was just twenty-one and called in when we were needing a bomb tech. We spoke here and there on the way to Jordan. He told me how he was recently engaged to his high school sweet heart, Jada. He was so excited. I could still see the shock on his face when we came under attack, and he was the first one shot. He was a good kid. Another good kid gone in an instant.

And I had watched my enemies die too, either through a scope or up close. Their faces still tormented my dreams at night. Every time someone died, I felt like I had been pushed out of a shuttle into the pitch darkness of space. I would float away from the light into the loneliness of nothingness. I knew that feeling well until my faith pulled me back in. However, I didn't know how many more times His grace would save me.

I sat outside her door like I did everyday with my face in my hands praying. My men would come around and ask what needed to be done, and I would hide my emotions and the praying from them. However, it was a nice reprieve when they came around. Today, Toms was on edge. He came up and sat with me while keeping his eyes on the Germans that were walking by.

"Something wrong?" I asked.

Tom's deadpan stare at our new friends was unwavering. "Eriksen, you know the drill. Trying to be courteous, professional."

I nodded while studying the same men that Toms watched. I finished his thought, "Always ready to neutralize everything at a moment's notice?"

"Yep."

"I'm doing the same. We'll never stop."

"Just a little more anxious, I guess."

"I hear ya."

"As I reported earlier, everything is moving along as written in history. But something about all that is still bothering me." He picked up some rocks near us and shifted them in his hand.

I noticed his nervous tension but added, "We know that since Arminius has achieved a higher officer status, he is still trusted by Varus. Did your reconnaissance tell you something else? Something you are not telling me?"

Toms sat there in silence. He was always the quietest of my team. He observed more often than he spoke. Every team needed someone with that type of personality. I never held it against him until now.

I shrugged. "Parker is dead. You verified it. You have reported nothing to me that has worried me."

His now stern face looked behind us where Kyla laid. "Just getting that same feeling I got when we traveled with the Senator."

"Noted. You read the Senator well then."

"Yea. But with all due respect, was it really a good idea keeping Kyla here among these people? She's no doubt contagious. Wasn't that Parker's plan?"

"It was, except he didn't expect someone with medical training to be here advising us on what to do and what not to do throughout her illness."

"Banks is great but..."

I cut him off. "We have followed every safety protocol when it came to Kyla's illness, including the old lady that has tended to her. The entire village knows that she is ill and has taken the proper precautions too." Then, I turned to him. His uneasiness was apparent by his rigid posture. I got that. I completely did, but he didn't need to know that. "I don't have to explain myself to you," I told him.

Toms set the rocks down and brushed off his hands. "I know. But we all know that you had a thing for her. I'm just making sure that you had thought all this through. That is all. No disrespect."

I tugged at the smock my German friends loaned me. Keeping my voice smooth and calm, I said, "None. But I would have done the same thing if it were any of you in there. You know that. No man left behind, remember? She earned her spot with us. Hell, she even managed to get the Romans to take out our target for us. Which is even better because you said it yourself, you and Memon witnessed the Romans burn all of Parker's things after the wedding. Less work on our part." I could tell something was changing in my men as the mission showed signs of ending. Our orders were to stop Parker. No one briefed us on another mission to do while we were stuck in the past. The only concern they had was that we stayed low and didn't change anything afterward.

"You're right," Toms said and stood up. "I guess I just needed to hear it from you. Putting all that aside, she shouldn't have to go through what she's going through now. It should be one of us in there. It was *our* job."

"I agree."

As he walked off, I thought about our orders and these men. I wouldn't have taken such a crazy mission like this with anyone else. No matter how much doubt crossed their minds, they would still always have my back.

I started biting my nails, another nervous habit. Memon came up looking back and forth between me and Toms. "Hey."

"Hello. Did that pretty girl over there find you those breeches? She keeps eyeing you." I asked and stood up to stretch.

"Lay off it. She's too young."

"I'm just saying because I have never seen you show that much leg." I put my hands on my hips and enjoyed watching him squirm. It was nice to pick on someone again. It took my mind off of Kyla.

"It's just my calves," Memon replied.

"If you say so. Have you taken inventory on things yet?"

He rubbed his dark beard. "Yes. We're a little low on brass for your rifle."

"I figured Banks got a little trigger happy."

"I guess. I was able to find some of the casings on the grounds back there in Venice afterward."

"None from the bodies?" I asked.

"Not yet. I'm not sure how much the Roman doctors will dig for them either. Everyone is viewing it as lightning from one of their gods. No one wants to touch the bodies yet. At least that is what I heard."

"Perfect. When you and Banks go back for your next recon, maybe then you can get to those bodies once the attention has died down."

Memon motioned to Kyla's hut. "Any news?"

"No."

Even though, I did not tell my men about my feelings for Kyla, they still acted uncomfortable around me. It all started after we realized that she had gotten sick. Memon asked nothing else and walked back to get his horse some water.

When everyone was out of sight, I sat back down and remained by her door still praying for a miracle. I knew it wouldn't come because Marburg was serious, especially in this time without the proper care. There was no way anyone could survive it. But did that mean my faith was still too weak? On that thought, I achingly stood up and headed to my rented hut across the way from Kyla's. I paid the old lady another coin for both mine and Kyla's boarding and went inside to sleep. All I got off were my boots before my weighted lids closed shut.

****

"Wake up, man." The next morning, Memon was standing inside my room trying to wake me up. I sat up to clear my eyes and to get my bearings. I checked for my gun and placed it in my holster under my shirt out of sight.

"What's wrong?"

"Banks and Toms spotted a Roman patrol on their rounds," Memon told me and stepped outside.

I followed him out. "Verdict?"

"The Chatti have already started packing to leave. They don't like it."

"Good, let's do the same and ASAP."

"Yes, sir. You know we will need to burn Kyla's hut with her body inside in order to stop the virus from spreading. I can do it, man. Say the word."

I cringed because we haven't verified that she was officially dead. Someone needed to check her pulse. I volunteered to do it. No way I was burning her alive.

As I was heading to the side of camp to speak with the Chatti clan, my Germanic landlord came across the path to me. "Eriksen, is your name Eriksen?"

"Yes."

"She's asking for an Eriksen. That must be you. She said the tall blonde, with bright blue eyes. And I know all the Chatti clan members. It must be you." She tilted her double chin down and smiled. "Sadly, I've been taking your money and never got your name."

"That's alright, but *she*? Who are you talking about?"

"The woman that has taken up residence in my hut!" she said in a put out way.

I ran back to the small hut by the solitary beech tree in the middle of the village. When I got there, I wasn't sure what to expect. I half thought the old lady was losing it. Then, I thought maybe I misunderstood her German because of her sharp accent. Either way, I arrived there preparing myself for the worse.

I opened the twig door and crossed the threshold that I hadn't crossed in five days. It took a second for my eyes to adjust but there she laid. Her eyes were closed and her skin was paler than I had ever seen it. But she still looked so beautiful. This sassy, petite thing still brought me to my knees, even in death. I spotted her holding the crucifix I gave her with one hand. The other graceful hand lay by her side. I reached up to check her pulse and brown eyes popped open.

"Eriksen?" She smiled weakly at me, and I thought I'd lost it.

"Kyla, you're alive."

"Yeah, I woke up earlier and the fever was gone." She feebly tried to sit up, but I stopped her.

"Take it easy. No rush."

"I can't believe the fever is gone. I thought I was a goner."

Banks came in and kneeled beside me to check her heart rate. "I heard what was going on. She has a good heart rate. Nice and steady. How is that possible?" he said looking at me.

"I don't know."

"Hey Banks." She gave him a big smile that didn't sit right with me.

"Are you okay?" Banks said back.

"I am now. I'm so thankful. It's like a miracle, right?"

Banks shook his head. "I don't know about miracles, Kyla. But we're glad you're okay."

She added, "I may disagree, because for the last few hours I've been thinking. I think I know what could have happened, though. It all makes sense now."

We shook our heads waiting.

She looked over at me now. Her eyes misty. "Remember I told you about my father, and how I didn't see him again after I turned eight?"

"Yes," I replied.

"There was something else Parker told me when he gave me the virus." She paused to take a sip of the water Banks brought her. "He told me he worked with my father and my father stole something from them. Parker didn't tell me what. I started thinking this morning. It's odd but the last night I saw my dad; he had gotten into a fight with my mom."

"We don't have to go over all this now. Let's just be happy you're alive." I touched her clammy face.

"No, listen. I don't know what the fight was over, but he took me into my room to talk to me. He said he needed to give me something, but it would be just like what I get at the doctor's office. I remember that because it was a strange gift to get." Her distant eyes glossed over.

Banks spoke up, "Kyla, if your father worked with Parker than it makes sense that he had access to the same biohazard chemicals."

"Do you think it was the antidote? Could I be immune?"

"Either from that or the fact that you just survived it. Your body either was already full of the antibodies, which explains why you didn't have any of the internal bleeding that usually accompanies hemorrhagic fever; or you have a healthy supply of them now." He said with relief.

I cleared my throat. "I agree."

She looked at me. "Geez, if I'm immune, it *is* a miracle. You were right about not believing in coincidences."

I just nodded. I didn't know what to say.

Then, Banks nudged me. "I guess you heard about the patrol?"

I shoved back up to my feet. "I have; let's take that outside."

Chapter 17

Han, the leader of the Chatti, seemed rather calm for being a traitor to the empire. "This is a nice day. I could do some good hunting today if not for those Romans," he told me while chewing on a pine needle.

"I would join you if we could."

A smirk passed over his face. "I bet you and your men are good hunters."

"That we are."

The older man faced me straight on. "When we get to my village, we should have a series of games. I am eager to see how the hunters fair from your homeland."

He was a competitive old man. This could prove to be interesting. "Deal."

"Deal?"

"I meant, I accept the challenge."

Han smiled with a few missing teeth and let out a jolly laugh. "I knew I was going to like you." Then, his face got serious and he continued, "We're packed up and ready to go. My son is not pleased about us waiting for you, but I know you are true to your word. So it will be worth it. We'll wait just a few more hours."

He seemed like an honorable man. I could use good allies in the days ahead. I knew eventually I would have to offer more in order to win more of their loyalty. Especially since I was not giving him back his son's bride. My thoughts drifted to Kyla; I wanted her. She was alive, and I couldn't help but think of how much I wanted her now. Maybe I was getting weak. I wasn't sure how my men would respond to that. I cut the distraction off. "We'll be ready."

As the chieftain walked off, I turned to Banks, my closest friend for years.

"We need to make a trade for a cart to carry Kyla. We'll try to leave within the hour."

"I'll look into it." Then he spoke low as we walked with our backs to the Chatti. "We've buried the excess coins we brought from the future and marked the locations, as instructed. I'll set a traveling sentry parameter of about one hundred feet. You don't trust these guys either?"

"Nope. I don't trust many in this time. Too much at stake."

"Got it. By the way, Toms traded out the batteries on the MBITRs."

"Good. As usual, only nighttime use. These Germans would notice. They are pretty observant."

We stopped by a tree and Banks dug into his pocket to pull out a cigar. "You know we could just go with the little walkie talkies. We are going to be spending a lot of time with these people and we'll be in a closer proximity of each other now. On top of that, we've got way more batteries for those."

I watched him light the little Cuban cigar. "Yea, let Toms know. That's good thinking. We'll be able to save our Lithium batteries. You never know what we'll need those for."

Banks blew the cigar smoke into the air and offered it to me. "Here. You need this more than I do."

"I'm good. I thought you quit all together."

"I never cold quit. I still have one from time to time. But these last few days, man I've gone through several. And I only brought ten."

I laughed and grasped his shoulder. "I don't blame you. It's been a ride, huh?"

"More so for you, you reject. I still can't believe those gladiator games. You kicked some tail back in that arena. You made us proud. I don't know if I could have done that."

"You could have. But yea, I guess I'm a little faster and stronger than you."

Banks put out the cigar on the bark of the tree to save it and laughed. "How would you know? You never had the balls to square off with this Texan in order to find out. Come to think of it, I would have taken out all those gladiators within the first five minutes."

"Keep thinking that." I looked around at the Germans finishing up their packing. "Let's get moving."

"Hooyah!" With that, Banks turned back toward the village. He was carrying his share of demons too, but I wouldn't choose any other man to be by my side.

****

I carried Kyla's frail body to the cart attached to my horse a little while later. The air was turning chillier, so I covered her up and mounted my horse. The Chatti tribe of five went on first to lead the way. I followed with Memon and Toms behind me.

The trek through the forest was not easy. I stopped the men more often than I should have to check on Kyla. She slept much of the way and didn't stir when I touched her face to check for a returning fever. Or maybe I just touched her face because I could. Either way, she was getting the rest she needed. I wasn't going to let anything happen to her again. I was going to get control of everything this time. No more mistakes. Especially not where she was concerned.

As we came into the Chatti village, I signaled for Banks to make camp. It was nice to finally be there and done riding. I made a small fire in the middle of the hut Han lent Kyla and I, and I laid her on the bed by it. She stirred and smiled at me. "Hey, you."

"Hello."

"Are you gonna rest?" she asked still smiling. I could tell she was glad to be alive and so was I. But what was she implying? To get my head straight since I had important things to do, I left her to relax alone. And I needed to get to work. Work was good, it kept my mind off of her and my wits about me. There was much to be done in order to secure us all a safe place.

I walked out to meet with the guys outside of the village. It was late in the day and getting chilly. Banks was sharpening his knife behind a tree and Toms was carving another one of his talismans. Memon came up behind me. "Cap., how is Kyla?"

"She's good."

"Listen up," I said to my men. "As you know, we only have about a year to make sure everything goes as written, and then we'll make a decision of how to proceed. You've all done well once again. I just wanted to let you all know that if by the end of the year, you decide to split off, start a family, or just live off the land in solitude; I will understand as long as you keep in touch."

Banks stopped sharpening his four-inch blade. "Why are we talking about this now?"

I walked up closer. "I *knew* we would be successful. I just never thought passed that."

Banks returned, "Doesn't matter, I'm staying around. I say we stay a team."

Memon nodded. "I agree. That was one thing from that meeting with those United Nations guys that stuck with me."

I turned to him. "What?"

"It would be better if we stuck together afterward. To make sure that we don't change anything without meaning to. Peer pressure, I guess."

"I agree," Toms said. "One question."

"Shoot."

"Can we fraternize? Memon needs to work things out with that young thing that followed us from the last village."

Everyone laughed but Memon.

Banks added, "Him *and* you, Eriksen. No harm in it. You and Kyla *are* in the same hut."

I stopped him, "We're not doing anything, Banks. I'm just staying close to watch her."

All the guys winked. "Uh huh."

Banks continued, "We have a whole year to wait. A little downtime with the ladies won't be so bad."

I smiled. "Honestly, I was already thinking it. As long as we keep the recon missions consistent and don't come across any problems."

Toms, being taller than Memon, brushed the top of Memon's head. "There you go, Memon. Go get her, tiger."

Everyone laughed again. It felt good. The men and I needed this.

I took a second to look at them in all their hide and leather Germanic clothing. Their loyalty was admirable, and I loved each and every one of them as a brother. It still sickened me about what I was ordered to do if any of them decided to use their knowledge and weapons for their own gain and threatened to change the future.

****

"You need to take a break." A few mornings later, I was still working on getting a good supply of firewood together when Kyla came out with her hair down and a blanket wrapped around her shoulders. She was addressing me like I was a kid. I could be agitated, but she looked good for the first time in days. She was starting to look like herself again. Compared to the Chatti women around, she looked amazing. I noticed some of the Chatti men would stop at the sight of her, but she kept her eyes on me.

She came up and plopped down across the fire from me. "You haven't slept."

"There's much to do," I spoke with a shrug of my tense shoulders.

"There is always a lot to do. You need to rest too."

I stretched my neck and continued sorting the wood while I talked. "I'm going to pull out my guns to clean tonight when everyone is asleep, so no one sees. You don't mind, do you?"

"Yes." And she giggled that sweet laugh that reached her eyes.

I smiled and moved my last log. "Good. The guys took care of their guns last night. This change in weather isn't good for them."

"So, what is the plan now?"

"We hang around. Make sure the Chatti meet up with Arminius for that final meeting the tribes have next year."

"Next year? I thought it was already starting."

"It is a long process. At least that's how it was written in history."

"So make sure Parker didn't affect anything?"

"Yes. We will be scouting the new Roman village nearby as the battle gets closer, to see what we can find out. Just to be sure."

"Makes sense. What about his bag? It wasn't with him when he died. There could be more vials."

"Yeah, I've talked to the men about that. Some of Parker's things were burned by the Romans after he died. We're hoping that bag was one of them. Banks and Toms will do some reconnaissance in the next few weeks back in Venice to see what we can find. If it doesn't turn up and the Germans still win the battle, then I'll feel the mission is officially a success. Overall and for the most part, we need to lay low and try to become a part of this tribe. Since the reality of this is that we're stuck here. We need to make a life here."

"How do we do that?" She says while looking around with apprehension. Her already tiny frame shook from the chill, and I noticed her weight loss from the last few days had made her even more frail. Then her eyes caught mine, and my heart instantly sped up.

I shook it off and looked to the muddy ground before answering. "Oh well... I've got someone I've got to fight." I stretched my arms in front of me and cracked my knuckles as she flinched.

Her cute nose wrinkled up, and her long lashed eyes flared up at me. "What? Not again. You men! You're pathetic. No, you're kidding right?"

"Afraid not. But I sized him up. I've got this."

She frowned. "Who is it?"

"Oh... your former fiancé."

She stood with her hands in fists and walked around the fire toward me. To my delight, she was angry and I liked it. "You're not doing it. I'm tired of you fighting."

I pulled her down to sit next to me. I smelled that same lilac smell she carried on her hair since the first night she rode in front of me to Jerusalem. It was intoxicating. "What are you going to do, fight him for me?"

"I can't believe this. I can't believe this! Do we ever get a break?" She was fired up, and her cheeks glowed red because of it.

I couldn't help it, I reached up for a strand of her hair. "Break to do what?" I asked drawing it out with each word very slowly. I was hoping for some kind of sign from her.

I followed her gaze as she looked around at the Chatti moms with their children walking around gathering supplies. "I guess it really isn't in the cards for us, is it? Like you said on the ship."

"I think it can be."

She turned and looked up at me with those seductive brown eyes. The light from the fire brought out the caramel specs around her pupils.

"We have some down time now." I paused thinking of how to proceed. "I'm going to be blunt. I want to do this right, Kyla. I want to marry you, now. No one has to know. We'll keep it a secret until after the battle, so it doesn't affect my men. The tribe here has a type of marriage ceremony we can do in private. I know it's not with a priest or rabbi, but it will be formal enough to be binding."

"No, we can't Eriksen." She looked down with sad eyes.

"Oh yeah, we can. I thought I lost you to that virus. And now we're here, resting. We could be doing other things." I grinned and willed her to agree.

"Look around Eriksen. Do you actually think we can set up house, have a family like these people, with everything going on and knowing what we know? How can we keep our minds in the game? We'll change. Things will change."

I grabbed her hand. "I still care about completing the mission, which I will do. But I care about you too. And we will finish the mission. I can promise you that. But I want you. You don't know how much I do. I'm not talking about having a family. Not anytime soon, believe me. I just want to do this right. I want you to be mine."

She shook her head. "Something changed for me too after I survived that virus. I prayed...Then, with the revelation about my father. Maybe I am here for a reason."

She withdrew her soft hand and looked down again. "I don't know. Let me think about it. Can you wait? Let me be sure. I need all this to sink in. I want to make that kind of decision when I'm in the right frame of mind." She looked back at me with those lovely, pleading eyes.

Her full rosy lips quivered, so I couldn't think of anything else. As I noticed more Chatti around us stop to watch, I reached for her tiny face and took it with both my hands. I drew her face to mine to claim her lips, then her mouth, to claim her in front of everyone. She was mine. And she didn't fight back.

I kissed her with the passion that had been building since the first day I met her on that elevator. As I tasted and embraced her, I couldn't stop. I didn't want anything in life but this moment right here, right now. But I'd respect her wishes and keep our relationship just like this until she was ready. I would definitely wait for her. I'd wait for her forever...

Oh and that thing about having to fight the Chief's son to have her, I made that up. I just love to get a rise out of her...

The End

About the Author

Jackie Anders has been an obsessed reader and lover of all fiction, ranging from sci-fi to historical, all her life. As a young adult growing up in Louisiana, she never missed an episode of X-Files, Stargate, or any of the Terminator movies. Anders is a mom of two teenagers, one elementary kiddo, and a part-husky dog named India. She is also married to a proud Texan and enjoys cheering on the Houston Astros!

Visit her at **jandersbooks.wordpress.com.**

Thank you so much for reading one of our **Sci-Fi/Fantasy** novels.
If you enjoyed our book, please check out our recommended title for your next great read!

War of the Staffs by Steve Stephenson & K.M. Tedrick

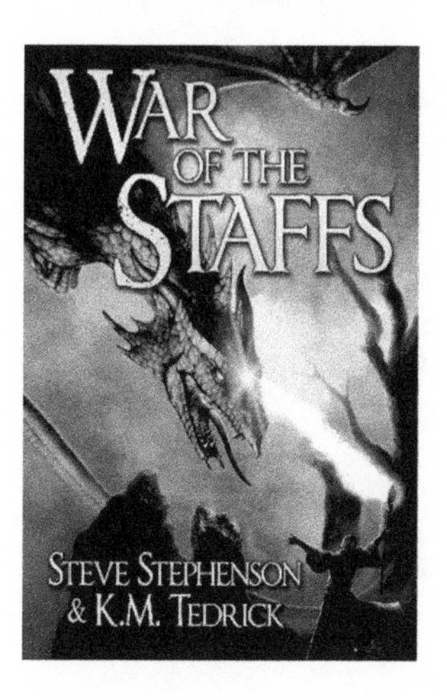

"Offers an enjoyable romp for high fantasy fans." –***KIRKUS REVIEWS***

CPSIA information can be obtained
at www.ICGtesting.com
Printed in the USA
LVHW091912291118
598532LV00004BA/489/P

9 781684 331642